This month we are proud to present ten classic stories from your most-loved Mills & Boon® Modern™ Romance authors!

This exclusive bestselling author collection includes:

Collect all ten!

D1382526

Miranda Lee is Australian, and lives near Sydney. Born and raised in the bush, she was boarding-school-educated, and briefly pursued a career in classical music before moving to Sydney and embracing the world of computers. Happily married, with three daughters, she began writing when family commitments kept her at home. She likes to create stories that are believable, modern, fast-paced and sexy. Her interests include meaty sagas, doing word puzzles, gambling and going to the movies.

Recent titles by the same author:

MASTER OF HER VIRTUE
CONTRACT WITH CONSEQUENCES
THE MAN EVERY WOMAN WANTS
NOT A MARRYING MAN

FUGITIVE BRIDE

BY
MIRANDA LEE

PROLOGUE

THE letter stood out because of its pink perfumed envelope.

Enid hesitated, then shrugged and opened it. As Gerard Woodward's confidential secretary she had permission to open all mail which came to the office unless it was clearly marked 'Private and Personal'. In fact, Gerard insisted upon it. He also insisted *she* decide and deal with everything not needing his individual attention. The head of Sunshine Enterprises did not want to be bothered with trivia.

Enid knew, however, from the first few words, that this was one letter she *shouldn't* have opened. But the damage had been done and there was no going back. She scanned the brief note all the way through, her chest becoming tighter with each word.

Dear Gerard,
By the time you read this I will have left you. Don't try to find me. You won't succeed. Even if you do, I won't come back to you, no matter what. Believe me when I say I never want to see you again. I overheard what you said to Steven last Sunday regarding your attitude towards love and marriage. And wives.
May God forgive you for what you've done to me, because I never will.

Leah

'Dear God,' Enid muttered.

She closed her eyes for a second, swivelled round in her chair and stood up. There was no use trying to hide her mistake in judgement. Gerard could not really blame her for opening the darned thing, though he might criticise her lack of feminine intuition. He would be really furious, however, at any delay in acquainting him with such a letter.

Gathering herself, she stepped up to the door which separated her office from her employer's and gave it her usual precise tap-tap.

'Yes,' came the curt reply.

Enid straightened her spine and marshalled a confident expression.

Gerard was a difficult and demanding boss at the best of times, a workaholic with a perfectionist personality. Failure was anathema to him; success his God. The man who would be king of Queensland's tourist industry was ruthless when crossed and given to caustic comments whenever anyone didn't come up to his impossibly high standards.

Fortunately, Enid was a top secretary, totally competent, cool in a crisis and unflappable under fire. During the eight years she'd held this job it had been rare for her to provoke her boss into criticising *her* work performance.

On the one occasion when she *had* been on the end of Gerard's cutting sarcasm Enid had been tempted to quit on the spot. She'd had a husband once with a nasty tongue and did not relish being on the end of anyone's temper these days.

But she was forty-six years old, and didn't fancy her chances on the open and very tough job market. Her qualifications were impeccable, but so were those of younger women who had more going for them than their secretarial skills.

Glamour had never been Enid's strong hand, and she looked every minute of her age. So she'd bitten her tongue at the time, while reminding herself Gerard paid her well enough to put up with the occasional blast.

But she didn't like the man. Not one bit.

Steeling herself against what was to come, she opened the door and stepped into the holy of holies.

He didn't look up, his attention all on some photographs he was studying. No doubt some cute coastal town was about to be besieged by offers its inhabitants couldn't refuse, after which their quiet, uncontaminated lives would never be the same again.

'What is it, Enid?' he said brusquely, still without looking up.

Enid almost relished giving him the damned thing. Serve him right, she thought.

'This letter came in the morning mail, Gerard,' she said coolly. 'I thought you would want to read it straight away.'

Now she had his attention, his dark head snapping up, a frown not marring his disgustingly handsome face.

'Who's it from?'

'Your wife.'

'Leah?' He could not have been more startled.

'I'm sorry, Gerard. It wasn't marked ''Private'', and there was no reason for me not to open it.' She came forward and handed the note across to him, thanking her lucky stars that the simple white paper it was written on was not as fancy as the pink envelope.

Butterflies crowded in Enid's stomach as her boss's piercing blue eyes immediately dropped to the note. She watched him read the 'Dear John' letter, watched as he tried to absorb his wife's rejection of him as a man and a husband.

A small shred of sympathy twisted Enid's heart. For she knew this had to be killing him. Gerard so hated to fail in anything.

Losing in a business deal was bad enough.

Losing his wife was something else...

Who would have believed it of Leah? To all appearances she was such a soft, trusting soul, a mere child when compared to her cynical and streetwise husband. Just twenty-one to his very sophisticated thirty-three. A babe in the woods. A lovely yet naive girl whom Gerard had clearly thought he could mould and train to be the sort of wife who would never give him any trouble: the type who stayed home and filled the roles of mother, lover and hostess to perfection, who never complained when he was late for dinner or had to fly away on business at a moment's notice, the type who loved her husband to distraction and blindly believed he loved her back, simply because he told her so.

Enid had cynically watched her employer play his

own roles to perfection so far. He'd been the perfect courtier, the perfect fiancé, the perfect new husband. Nothing had been too good for his bride. He'd showered her with every luxury money could provide. He'd seemingly showered her with his personal attention as well...up to a point.

Not that they'd been married long. Just over nine months.

Enid had been waiting for the rot to set in, for Gerard to show his true colours. And it seemed he had.

For ages he just sat there and stared at the paper. When his hands started shaking, he crumpled the note into a crushed ball and leapt to his feet, his face flushing angrily.

'You read this?' he growled, glaring at Enid.

She nodded.

He swore, then whirled to stalk over to the far window which overlooked the Brisbane river. But he didn't look at the view. With hands still shaking, he unfolded the crushed note and read it again.

Suddenly he spun back to face Enid, his blue eyes glittering as they did when he got the bit between his teeth over something and was about to run with it.

'Do you have the envelope this came in?'

Enid nodded again, but she was quaking in her sensible shoes. One look at that envelope and he might question her discretion in opening it.

'Get it for me,' he snapped. 'And get Burt Lathom on the phone.'

Enid's eyes rounded. Burt Lathom was a private investigator Gerard used sometimes when he needed to find some dirt on one of his competitors. The man was thorough and usually came through with the goods.

'Well, don't just stand there gawking at me,' Gerard snarled. 'That won't bring Leah back, will it?'

'But...she said she didn't want to come back,' Enid was driven to protest for a fellow female.

'The only thing Leah wants,' Gerard ground out with his usual one-eyed stubbornness, 'is to be my wife. Unfortunately, she has totally misunderstood some things I said to a man who was distressed over his divorce at the time. When Burt finds her I'll make her see that. Now hop to it, woman. Time is a-wasting. I have an important business dinner this coming Saturday night and my wife is going to be there, by my side, as usual!'

Enid had no choice but to do as she was told, but she did so resentfully, hoping all the while that Burt Lathom would be unsuccessful. Leah was a sweet girl and deserved better than to be hoodwinked by the likes of Gerard Woodward.

Handsome he might be. And clever. And rich. But there wasn't a soft-hearted cell in his entire body. He was a ruthless predator who was incapable of really loving a woman. He was a user and a manipulator. A conscienceless cynic.

Unfortunately, Leah loved him. Even Enid had seen that. She fairly glowed whenever he looked at her. In all likelihood she still loved him, despite that letter.

Enid prayed Gerard would never find his fugitive bride. For God knows what would happen to her, if and when he did.

CHAPTER ONE

SIX months.

Leah leant against the mast of the old pearling lugger, dragged in a deep breath of sea air, then let it out slowly.

Six months...

Time to relax at last, perhaps? Time to stop looking over her shoulder and expecting Gerard to be standing there?

He hadn't found her yet.

Which still surprised her.

Admittedly, she'd planned her escape well, had known how imperative it was not to leave anything for him to go on. She'd taken nothing which belonged to her life as Mrs Gerard Woodward. Not her gleaming white Porsche. None of the glamorous clothes hanging in her massive walk-in wardrobe. Certainly none of her credit cards.

Only cash. And then only as much as she needed.

Leah had wanted nothing from her marriage except escape.

She hadn't gone home to Hidden Bay, not even for a moment, because that would have been the first place Gerard would look. She'd fled to Townsville where her brothers had organised for her to help a friend take a racing boat to Indonesia, after which she'd crewed on another racing boat, returning it to its rich owners on the Riviera.

Now she was back in Australia, but in a place Gerard would not think to look.

Leah closed her eyes momentarily, a tremor racing through her. She might have physically escaped, but it would be a long time before she found emotional escape. Gerard was out of sight, but would he ever be dispelled from her mind? Or ejected from her traitorous body?

She still dreamt of him at night, disturbing dreams in which Gerard was inevitably making love to her as only he could. She would always wake just as the act was being consummated, leaving her hot and trembling from a desire as real as the dream had seemed.

How long, she agonised, before the fires Gerard had carefully and callously stoked within her were extinguished? How long before she stopped needing what he'd made her addicted to? Him, every night in her bed. Him, making her respond, even when she didn't want to.

Leah shuddered at the memory of her appalling weakness for the man, even *after* her shocking discovery that Sunday.

How could she have let him make love to her that night when she'd *known* what he was? Worse, how could she have found pleasure in it?

She shuddered again, despising herself anew. It was wicked for a man to have such power over a woman. There again, Gerard *was* wicked.

Leah sighed. He'd looked anything but wicked that day eighteen months ago when he'd come striding

down the pier at Hidden Bay, wearing dazzlingly
white shorts and T-shirt, perfect foils for his deeply
olive skin and jet-black hair. Perfect vehicles to dis-
play his tall, superbly muscled body.

Leah was not to learn till after their marriage how
hard Gerard worked on that body, witnessing herself
the gruelling daily weight routine he put himself
through in his private gym to achieve such physical
perfection.

He didn't have to work on his face, however. It had
been born perfect, with classically sculptured features,
a mouth to die for and come-to-bed blue eyes.

Leah would never forget the instant lurching in her
stomach when she'd looked up and seen that handsome face for the first time...

'Hi, there,' he said, coming to a halt near the prow of
her brothers' fishing charter boat and giving her a very
slow and sexually charged once-over. 'You for hire,
honey?'

She just gaped at him, colour flooding up her throat
and into her cheeks.

'The boat, darling,' he drawled, his eyes gleaming
with wry amusement. 'I meant the boat.'

'Oh.' She straightened from where she'd been
swabbing the deck with a mop and bucket.

Of course he meant the boat! How could she have
possibly imagined a man like him meant otherwise,
even for a moment? Good grief, she must look a sight,
with perspiration running down her face, her hair half
falling down, and her shorts and top soggy from the

water she'd been sloshing around in somewhat of a temper.

'Hot and bothered' did not begin to describe her at that moment, her discomfort not helped by this amazingly good-looking man who kept staring at her.

Not at her flushed face, however. At her...

A panicky downward glance confirmed that one of her braless breasts was clearly outlined against a patch of damp cotton, the startlingly erect nipple making a real exhibition of itself.

Embarrassment snapped Leah's hands together across her chest, the inadequately shielding handle of the mop clasped between them.

'Yes, it is,' she said, hating her high-pitched voice. 'But Mike and Pete aren't here at the moment.'

'Mike and Pete?'

Leah gulped down the lump in her throat and gathered a modicum of composure. 'My brothers. They own the boat. They should be back soon. They went trail-bike riding with some mates early this morning.' Which was the only time to go, before the heat of the day. If living on the Queensland coast had one major drawback it was the sometimes debilitating humidity.

'And left you to do all the dirty work, I see.'

Leah didn't like the criticism in the stranger's words. No one was allowed to criticise her brothers except herself! 'Not at all,' she defended. 'They work hard and deserve a morning off. It's just that I have an aversion to washing floors. Any other cleaning job I'll do quite willingly. But not floors.'

'In that case I promise never to ask you to wash

my floors.' He smiled widely at her, his blue eyes dancing.

Leah found herself smiling back, even while her heart fluttered and her stomach flipped over. Never had a man affected her like this. There again, never had a man like this come to Hidden Bay before.

They didn't call the bay 'Hidden' for nothing. The pear-shaped cove was well disguised from the sea by overlapping headlands, high hills and thick vegetation. A small community of whalers had settled there a hundred years before, the protected bay a perfect sanctuary for their boats during the cyclone season.

Nowadays it only boasted about two hundred permanent residents. The electricity had finally been connected a few years back, and last year they'd celebrated the first sealed road leading out of the place, finally giving the world access without having to use a four-wheel drive.

Despite such stunning progress, not many outsiders knew of Hidden Bay's existence, and those who did guarded its location like a guilty secret. There were several families from down south who came up for their holidays during the cooler months, putting up with the lack of facilities in exchange for no pollution, warm waters and perfect peace and quiet. They'd begun arriving last week.

Despite his casual gear, the man standing before Leah didn't look as if he was attached to those intrepid holidaymakers, who were salt-of-the-earth types, people who liked nothing better than to sit around a campfire after a lazy day fishing, drinking a tinnie or two and discussing the ones who'd got away.

Leah suspected this fellow was used to more sophisticated pastimes. There was something about the
cut and grooming of his thick black wavy hair which
shouted money. That gold watch on his wrist looked
very expensive as well, as did the wraparound sunglasses dangling from his left hand.

She wondered what on earth he was doing here,
and why he wanted to hire her brothers' boat. There
seemed only one likely explanation.

'I suppose you want Mike and Pete to take you
deep-sea fishing,' she said, more of a statement than
a question. They did get the odd marlin-manic mil-
lionaire finding his way to their boat charter business,
hoping that the less-fished waters would provide some
spectacular catches. But in truth the ocean just off
Hidden Bay rarely gave up its really big fish. But
there were loads of coral trout, red emperor and snap-
per to be had.

'No, I'm not interested in fishing,' he said.

'Well, we don't do holiday cruises, if that's what
you're looking for. Only fishing charters.'

'That's all right. I don't want a holiday cruise,
either,' he said, his gaze travelling over her from head
to toe a second time.

Leah had always had to put up with a degree of
male attention, being tall, blonde and pretty, with a
good figure. Normally she didn't mind, except when
the male in question was being really objectionable.
Her over-protective older brothers, however, always
went ballistic.

Ever since their parents had passed away they'd
assumed the roles of her guardians with a vengeance,

being incredibly strict for two modern lads who thought nothing of the fact that they were both sleeping with *their* girlfriends—both of whom weren't much older than Leah.

If a local lad had the temerity to ask their kid sister out, he was issued with such dire warnings that Leah's relationships with the opposite sex never lasted long. Never got off the ground, really.

She was a week short of twenty and still a virgin.

Not that she minded her inexperience. She'd never thought she was missing out on anything. In truth, she'd never felt the slightest inclination to go beyond kissing and hand-holding with any male.

Till now…

'Well, what do you *want*, then?' she asked, mildly exasperated and more than a little agitated by the alien feelings flooding through her.

'Just to have a good look around the bay,' he said coolly, even while his eyes kept eating her up. 'I'd heard about this place, but had no idea it had such hidden…treasures.'

Leah could hardly believe the messages he was sending, both with his smouldering blue gaze and this last astonishing *double entendre*. She stared back at him, beyond blushing now, beyond anything but savouring the seductive thought that this incredibly handsome, suave, sexy, assured man seemed to be finding her as irresistibly attractive as she found him.

'My name's Gerard, by the way,' he said, climbing over onto the deck of the boat and holding out his large tanned hand. 'Gerard Woodward.'

'Leah,' she returned breathlessly, and placed her

own slender and slightly shaking fingers within the confines of his longer and much stronger grip. 'Leah…um…um…' Panic set in as her befuddled brain blankly scoured her memory for her own silly surname!

'Leah Um-Um,' he said teasingly. 'What an interesting name.'

The blush rushed back, hotter than ever.

'It's White,' she blurted out at last. 'Leah White.' Dear Heaven, but why did she have to make a fool of herself in front of him?

'Well, Leah White,' he said, his smile soft and warm, 'I think that's a very nice name and suits you admirably. But Woodward would be better.'

'Woodward?'

'That's *my* name. Have you forgotten it already? What fun it will be to tell our children that when their mother met their father she forgot her own name, and then his.'

'Our *children*?' she choked out.

'You do want children, don't you?' he asked, for all the world as if it was a serious question.

'I… I…'

His smile became both admiring and indulgent as he lifted her fingers to his mouth. 'I can see I'll have to make all the important decisions in our marriage. But that's all right by me,' he murmured as he kissed each fingertip in turn. 'I've always believed that a man is head of his family and king of his castle.'

Leah snatched her hand away from him. 'You're crazy as a loon!'

'Not at all,' he returned, without turning a hair. 'In

fact, I could give you a hundred references testifying to my sanity. But I appreciate I *am* rushing you a little. I promise to slow down if you promise to have dinner with me tonight. Ah…these must be your brothers now. Mike and Pete, did you say?'

She nodded dumbly, and watched while he charmed her two normally wary big brothers as effortlessly as he had charmed her.

He explained he was a property developer from Brisbane who was interested in buying some land in the area—with a view to building a small but exclusive resort. Any quibbles or qualms the boys raised about such a development were quickly waylaid by Gerard's ready reassurances. Anything he built would fit right into the environment and not spoil the area. It would also bring some much needed money into the local community. He would guarantee it!

By the end of the day neither Mike nor Pete made any objection whatsoever when Gerard politely asked their permission to take Leah to dinner. He wasn't given a single warning. Not one!

As it turned out, he didn't need one. For he didn't lay a finger on Leah, just a small peck goodnight on her cheek.

She lay awake into the wee small hours, thinking of him…

And so began their whirlwind courtship, Gerard sweeping Leah off to the altar barely three months after their first meeting.

She went to his bed on their wedding night still a virgin.

Not that she'd wanted to be. The moment she'd set eyes on Gerard he'd stirred a sensuality in her she hadn't known she possessed. But he'd wanted to wait, he'd told her.

At the time she'd thought that was so sweet. Now she realised it was all part of his Prince Charming act. In reality he'd probably had some other woman on the side, catering to his carnal needs, while he made silly Leah wait. By the time the wedding had come along she'd been consumed by the most excruciating sexual tension, a ready slave for whatever he wanted, whenever he wanted it.

Prince Charming indeed! He was the devil incarnate!

Leah sometimes wondered what would have happened if she hadn't decided to go for a walk in the garden that fateful night, if she'd never overheard that appalling conversation. The realisation that she would still be going along blithely and blindly as Mrs Gerard Woodward brought mixed feelings. Maybe it would have been better if she'd never found out. She'd been happy, hadn't she?

Not entirely, she was forced to concede. Oh, yes, Gerard had given her everything she could possibly want. He'd spoiled her outrageously.

And it had been wonderful for a while. Gerard had swept her into a world she hardly knew existed, a sophisticated glamorous world of designer gowns, dinner parties and decadently expensive restaurants. She'd been agog with excitement over it all for the first few months.

But eventually her privileged and pampered lifestyle had begun to pall a little. She'd become bored with having nothing to fill her days but dress-fittings and hair appointments. Her only activity had been to make herself beautiful for the evenings she spent with her husband.

Once the honeymoon was over, she'd rarely seen Gerard during the day, and he worked six days a week. Sundays hadn't been much better. He'd spent so much time on the telephone, even in the car when they were driving somewhere. Mobile phones, she believed, were a menace.

When she'd mildly complained over breakfast one day of her loneliness and boredom, Gerard had suggested charity organisations, flower-arranging classes and cordon bleu cookery courses. When she'd hinted at a baby instead, he'd vetoed that for another year at least. He wanted her all to himself for a while, he'd said.

That night he'd come home with two dozen red roses and made love to her for hours.

Looking back, Leah could well understand why she hadn't been really content! Gerard had reduced her to nothing but a glorified mistress and hostess. He hadn't discussed his business with her, except in scant detail. She knew nothing much about his past, or even his present, except what he'd chosen to tell her. Which wasn't much. She'd had no friends of her own. No life of her own, except as Gerard's wife.

It had been her growing discontent which had driven her into the garden that fateful evening. One of Gerard's business colleagues had come over for dinner, and, true to form, after coffee Gerard had taken him into his study to talk business, leaving Leah at a loose end. As usual.

So she'd decided to walk down to the garden seat which overlooked the Brisbane river. Water always soothed her. It was a very pretty spot at night, looking across from their exclusive position on Kangaroo Point to the Story Bridge, and the lights of the city beyond.

She'd left the house by a side door, and had been walking along a path not far from the study when the open French doors and the stillness of the sultry evening had caused Gerard's voice to carry far beyond the room.

'You made a big mistake marrying a woman you loved so madly, Steven. Such passion destroys a man's brain cells. And his judgement. Marriage should be approached like a business deal. With lots of cool thought and calculated research.'

On hearing those first shocking comments, Leah became riveted to the spot. But there were more shocks to come.

'There are two types of women,' Gerard continued. 'Soft and hard. The givers and the takers. The first wants to love and *be* loved in return. The second wants everything else. Believe me when I tell you that these days the soft ones are getting rarer. You have to get them young, before they're contaminated by other men. And life.

'Take Leah for instance. She was only nineteen when I met her and had had no serious boyfriends before me. Naturally, she wasn't from the city. Generally speaking, city girls are bad news. I knew from the moment I met Leah that she was just what I was looking for. Perfect wife material in every way. Innocent, sweet, beautiful. A natural giver.'

'And very much in love with you,' Steven remarked drily.

'Still is,' Gerard pronounced with a casual arrogance that took Leah's breath away.

'Of course, we've only been married a short time,' he went on. 'But I have no intention of ever becoming too complacent where Leah is concerned. You know what happens when you neglect a business. Before you know it the damned thing folds. I gave up a whole month for our honeymoon, and still pour a lot of time and money into my beautiful new bride. I don't neglect her in the bedroom and I give her every material thing any woman could possibly desire, in return for which she gives me what every man wants. Complete love and loyalty.'

'But don't you love her, Gerard?' came Steven's troubled question.

'Love wears best on a woman,' came his coldly cynical reply. 'As I said before, a man who loves is weaker for it. It makes him stupid. And vulnerable. The last thing a woman wants is a husband who's weak, stupid and vulnerable. In the ends she falls out of love with such a fool and leaves him for another, stronger individual. Of course, I'm not saying you don't *tell* them you love them. Amazing what those three little words can do for a marriage. I don't let a day go by without telling Leah how much I love her.'

'That sounds awfully callous, Gerard...'

'Not at all. It works, Steven. You won't find my marriage ending in divorce, you mark my words.'

Leah had certainly marked them. *All* of them.

What a pity she hadn't had the courage to throw them in his face, personally!

She'd been going to confront him that night, as soon as Steven had left the house. But the wretched man had stayed for ages, till her own misery had forced her to go upstairs to bed.

Not that she'd slept. Midnight had found her lying wide awake in bed, tensely listening to Gerard's footsteps on the stairs.

'Waiting up for me, darling?' he said on entering the room. 'How sweet,' he murmured, smiling softly down at her as he undressed.

Leah watched him, dry-mouthed, her stomach swirling with a mixture of distress and dismay. She felt sickened by the situation, and her foolishness in being taken in by him so easily.

And yet, how could she have known what he was? He'd always been so incredibly good to her, had fulfilled all her romantic dreams, especially in bed. No man could have been a better lover. Or more considerate.

Her mind was whirling with all these thoughts when he slipped into bed beside her. Her mouth opened to say something, only to be covered by his in a gentle kiss. Much more gentle than was his usual style. Leah hoped that meant he wasn't going to continue, that it was just a goodnight kiss. But it seemed stopping was not on Gerard's mind. Soon, it wasn't on her mind, either.

Afterwards, she lay there, stunned, shattered. How could she have let him? And how could she possibly have found pleasure in it?

It was then that she knew she had to remove herself completely from his corruptive physical presence. She had to flee. If she confronted him with the truth—that she'd overheard what he'd told Steven in the study after dinner—he would find some way to explain it, to convince her that he didn't really believe what he'd said, that he did really love her.

Gerard was a natural born salesman. A clever and convincing talker. He could almost make people believe black was white when he wanted to. On top of that he would surely use sex against her, seducing her to his will, corrupting her with the pleasures of the flesh.

Leah believed if she let him do that, she would be lost. She could bear a lot of things in life, but she could not bear to live a lie. Gerard's love had meant the world to her. Dear heaven, it *was* her world! She'd given up everything for him. Her family and friends. Her home. Her beloved ocean.

All for nothing. An illusion. A trap.

On the Monday, she made her secret plans to flee the marriage, and this man who had such terrible power over her—demonstrating that power again that night, despite Leah finding what she hoped was the perfect excuse to be left alone. A migraine.

Her claim of a headache, however, brought nothing but solicitous offerings of painkillers and an aromatherapy massage. Admittedly, it had been a very long, very sensual massage. In the end she succumbed to those knowing hands, despising herself all the while she was wallowing in her husband's erotic expertise. When she sobbed afterwards in his arms, he actually thought her still in pain, and was so apologetic she almost thought she had to be mistaken about him.

But that was just desperation talking, silly Leah not wanting to believe she could still love and want any man who could speak of marriage—*their* marriage— as he had that Sunday evening.

The final night she spent in their marital bed did not include any further humiliation. Leah could not have borne it. She'd come to the difficult decision to take the initiative in the bedroom that last night, thereby salvaging what little pride and self-respect she had left. Better she accept the inevitable with some dignity than act like some ninny of a victim who could not help herself.

So she climbed into their bed naked and reached for him first, startling him. Not once during their marriage had she done that. Perversely, he'd seemed very pleased. He didn't realise her actions were inspired by desperation. And despair.

It was ironic that his subsequent lovemaking carried a sweet tenderness Leah had never previously experienced in his arms. She responded to that tenderness, even more than she had to his passion the previous two nights.

Gerard would never know how much he had lost in losing her. She would have devoted her life to him, if only he'd loved her back. Instead, he'd reduced her to nothing but a shell of a woman, tormented by thoughts of what might have been, tortured by what her marriage had actually been.

A cruel, cynical, cold-blooded sham.

'Got the food and drink ready, Leah?'

Leah spun round, the sea breeze whipping her long honey-blonde hair across her face. 'Yes, Alan. Everything's ready,' she called back.

'Good girl. Hold the fort while I collect tonight's party,' he said, nodding towards the distant figures on the beach.

Leah shaded her eyes with her hands and peered to shore. She knew they had a booking for six, but not the ages or sexes of the people. It looked like two couples, a single woman and a single man. You could usually guess their status by the way they stood, either in close pairs or out on their own.

'Won't be long.' Alan undid the rope, jumped into the Zodiac dinghy and fired the outboard motor. Within seconds the small craft was speeding across the water towards the beach, its flat bottom slapping across the tops of the waves, salt spray flying everywhere.

He was a bit of a cowboy, was Alan.

He was also the captain and owner of *The Zephyr*, an old pearling lugger built back in the 1920s. Alan had bought it a few years back, and now made a tidy living carrying tourists up and down the West Australian coast, his speciality being sunset cruises along Cable Beach during the Broome holiday season, which ran from late May till early September.

Six weeks ago Leah had heard on the yachtie grapevine in Darwin that the owner of *The Zephyr* wanted a female deck-hand, someone young and attractive who knew about sailing boats and who could handle the hostessing part of the job. So she'd applied and been immediately offered the job. Once she'd assured herself Alan didn't think he was hiring himself a live-in lover for the duration, she'd had no hesitation in accepting his offer.

He'd been a perfect gentleman so far. Not so perfect a gentleman with *other* members of her sex, however. A steady stream of women had trailed through the captain's cabin since *The Zephyr's* arrival in Broome.

Alan had this thing for older women, it seemed. He had no trouble reeling them in, either. Around thirty-five, he wasn't what Leah would have called handsome. But it seemed his long blond hair, bronzed body and soulful brown eyes always got the women in, especially the ones around forty.

Leah wondered if the unattached woman standing alone on that beach might be in Alan's required age bracket. It was a distinct possibility, and she watched him angle the boat further in than usual.

The wide flat tides around Cable Beach made it impossible to use a regular dinghy to pick up their clients. Most times, Alan still couldn't get the Zodiac right in, and the people had to wade out a bit into the water. He only made this kind of extra effort when a lady he fancied was concerned.

Leah shook her head. Some men were devils when it came to women and sex, she decided. She wanted nothing more to do with that type. Not ever!

Alan turned the Zodiac—now lined with people—

and headed back towards the lugger, going as fast as ever. Show-off, Leah thought wryly as she moved to stand at the side railing, ready to help everyone aboard. Twenty seconds later, the small craft was close enough for her to make out the various eager and expectant faces.

When her gaze moved to the man sitting alone at the back her eyes flung wide, her heart missing more than a beat.

'Oh, no,' she groaned. 'No, it *can't* be.'

But there was no mistaking that handsome face. Or those penetrating eyes.

Her husband had found her.

There was no escape this time, not unless she flung herself into the depths of the Indian Ocean.

CHAPTER TWO

HER heart started thudding. Blood began roaring through her head. As did a whole host of furious thoughts.

How dared he pursue her like this?

Six months had gone by. Six long, miserable months. She'd just begun to feel safe. Just begun to feel as if she might survive without him. And what does he do? Turns up like a bad penny!

What in God's name did she have to do to make good her escape? She'd fled the damned country, hadn't she? Lived on the high seas. Worked menial jobs in far-flung harbours around the world for months before daring to return to Australia. Even then, she'd only stayed because this job had been in such a remote corner of the country. Gerard had always said he had no interest in any other state except Queensland.

How had he found her? Had some wretched tourist from Brisbane recognised her and reported back to him?

No, she decided. That wouldn't have been likely. People from Brisbane rarely holidayed in Broome.

He'd found her the way men like him always found people. He'd hired some professional to hunt her down, to track her like some wretched criminal on the run. And now that she'd been found, he'd come himself to hound her into going back to him.

Well, she wouldn't! Never! Ever! He would have to hog-tie her and drag her back to Brisbane. She would never voluntarily go back.

Leah had thought she'd be afraid if and when Gerard caught up with her, thought she'd be terrified of the wicked power he had over her. She wasn't. She was simply livid!

Her eyes glared daggers at him as the Zodiac pulled alongside. She didn't notice Alan glaring at *her* when she failed to take the rope and secure the boat to the lugger. All she saw was Gerard, staring back at her with a blank expression, as though he had no idea why she was scowling at him with such ill-concealed fury.

His lack of sensitivity only infuriated her further.

Alan finally communicated his own frustration with Leah by throwing the rope into her hands.

Reluctantly, she turned her attention to the job at hand, securing the boat to the side of the lugger. Her smile was stiff as she introduced herself, then proceeded to help the party aboard, finding out in the process that the first couple were called David and Dawn, and the second Geoff and Peggy. All four were around sixty and obviously good friends, confiding in Leah within seconds that they'd all retired recently and had been travelling around Australia together for several weeks.

The single woman's name was Sandra. She was fortyish, as Leah had guessed. Quite attractive too, she supposed, if you liked plump blondes who wore too much make-up and gushed over everything. The avid glances Alan was giving Sandra's womanly derriere as she stepped onto the deck seemed to indicate he did.

'This is just too too exciting!' Sandra enthused, one hand fluttering up to her throat as she gazed around with seemingly enthralled eyes.

'Watch your step,' Leah warned on sighting her high-heeled sandals. 'The deck is smooth and can be slippery.'

'Don't you worry, sweetie,' she said smugly. 'I won't fall. These shoes and I have gone to the top of Ayer's Rock together. They're like part of me.'

Leah could believe it. She'd met other women like Sandra on her travels. They looked all fluff on the surface, but underneath were tough as an old boot. They were survivors, the Sandras of this world. Not like the Leahs, the silly, soft, sentimental Leahs...

Leah gathered all her newly found courage and turned to face Gerard. He rose from where he'd remained sitting at the back of the small craft, his face now the picture of puzzlement.

Did he think he was fooling her with that stupid expression? She knew why he'd come. To get her back! The almighty Gerard Woodward could not be allowed to be seen to be a failure. His marriage could not possibly end in desertion, or, even worse... divorce!

Her temper rose another notch, so much so that when Gerard took a step towards the front of the Zodiac she was ripe and ready for him.

'Not you,' she spat at him, jabbing her right index

finger towards his chest. 'You can just stay right there and let Alan take you back to the beach!'

He blinked while Alan simply gaped. Leah was aware of Sandra gasping behind her.

'Good God, Leah,' her boss spluttered. 'What's got into you?'

'I'll tell you what's got into me. That person there,' she ground out, pointing straight at Gerard's cold-blooded heart, 'isn't the innocent tourist he's pretending to be. He happens to be my ex-husband. He isn't here for a simple cruise. He's here to make trouble. Believe me when I tell you he's a sneaky, conniving conman and you can't believe a word he says!'

Alan gave the sneaky, conniving conman a darkly suspicious glance. 'Is that true? Are you Leah's ex-husband?'

'No,' came the cool reply.

Leah laughed. 'Okay, so you want to be literal! Legally, you *are* still my husband, I guess. But I walked out on our ghastly marriage six months ago, Alan, and haven't seen this mockery of a husband since that day. In my book, that makes him about as *ex* as you can get.'

'I'm not her husband, either,' the mockery said.

Now it was Leah's turn to gape.

'Not my husband!' she finally snapped. 'What kind of game are you playing, Gerard? You can't get a divorce in this country under twelve months, no matter how much money and connections you've got. I know. I asked.'

'I'm not your husband because I'm not Gerard. But

I can understand your mistake. I'm Gerard's twin brother…Gareth.'

Leah was speechless. But not for long.

'Gerard doesn't have a twin brother,' she argued. 'He doesn't have a brother at all. Period! He's an only child.'

'Is that what he told you?' came the calm query.

'Yes!'

'What else?'

'What do you mean, what *else*?'

'I mean…regarding his family.'

'He doesn't have any family. His mother and father died some years back.'

'Our father did. But our mother is alive and well and living in New York. I spoke to her only yesterday on the telephone.'

Leah's mouth dropped open.

'Well, you did say you couldn't believe a word your husband said,' Alan pointed out with merciless logic.

'Yes, but…but…' Leah's frantic gaze scanned the man standing before her, raking him from head to toe to see if there was any visible evidence this was not Gerard. Since he was dressed casually, in pale grey shorts and a navy and white striped top, she could see quite a bit of him.

He looked leaner than Gerard, she finally conceded. And not quite as muscly. He looked older, too, with deeper lines etched around his mouth and eyes—eyes which at that moment were looking at her with a most irritating composure, as though he was patiently waiting for the truth of his identity to sink in.

'I think you owe the man an apology, Leah,' Alan grated out.

Leah glanced up into the man's eyes, eyes which were identical to Gerard's. They met hers levelly and quite blandly. Despite that, something decidedly sexual curled in her stomach.

Gerard had always been able to turn her on, just by looking at her. No way could another man—not even an identical twin—reproduce what Gerard could make her feel. Such a possibility was beyond belief.

'Never in a month of Sundays,' she bit out, 'will I apologise, because I know I'm right. This man is my husband, Gerard Woodward, no matter what clever lies he trots out.'

'Good grief, Leah!' Alan exclaimed exasperatedly. 'Why on earth would he say he's your husband's brother if he wasn't?'

'I don't know.' Unless it was to trick her into letting her guard down with him. Maybe he was plotting to kidnap her, or some equally appalling plan. She would put nothing past Gerard. She knew the real man now, knew what he was capable of.

Where once she'd thought him wonderfully strong and decisive, she now knew he was cold-bloodedly ruthless. His veins ran with ice, not blood. His silver tongue spouted lies with superb ease. My God, when she thought of the thousands of times he'd told her he loved her! Every morning before he left for work. Every time he'd made love to her.

Made love? she thought sneeringly. Such a description was a joke! Gerard had never made love to her.

He'd seduced her. Manipulated her. Used her. Love had never come into the equation.

Nausea swirled in her stomach at the renewal of this bitter realisation. All lies. The man was a total lie. This crazy claim about a twin brother was a lie!

Hatred burnt in her eyes as she glared up at him.

'I'm not him,' he reiterated, in a voice so unlike Gerard's that she was momentarily thrown. Suddenly his eyes were not Gerard's, either. They were soft, and sad. Gerard had a wide range of expressions, but soft and sad was not one of them.

Still…faith in one's husband, and one's own judgement, once lost was not easily restored.

Leah hardened her heart against that treacherous weakness of hers to simply believe what she was told.

'Do you honestly think you can fool me a second time?' she threw at him in her agony and fury. 'You're Gerard and nothing and no one can convince me otherwise. So, I repeat, you either go back to that beach or I will. I'll swim if I have to!'

Alan sighed his own frustration. 'For pity's sake, Leah, you're paranoid. It's perfectly clear this chap isn't your husband. Why won't you believe him?'

'It's all right,' the man himself said. 'I fully understand the young lady's attitude, especially since she is unfortunate enough to be my brother's wife. Gerard's not a very nice person. He can be, in fact, a bastard of the first order. But I repeat…Leah, is it?…I am not Gerard. I'm nothing like him, except in looks, which is something I can do little about. I'm sorry if I have upset you. Truly sorry.'

Leah could only stare. An *apology*?

Apologies were anathema to Gerard. He gave reasons for his actions. Sometimes excuses. But never apologies.

Maybe—just maybe—this person standing before her *wasn't* Gerard.

But only *maybe*. Leah was not about to rush into believing anything any more. Not where her husband was concerned.

Her eyes remained hard upon him. And sceptical.

The man who claimed he wasn't her husband shrugged. 'Perhaps you *should* take me back to the beach,' he directed towards Alan. 'I don't want to spoil the cruise for everyone else.'

'Certainly not!' Alan replied. 'If Leah has a problem with your being on this cruise then *she* can be the one to go back to the beach. *I* believe you're not her ex, even if she doesn't. No man would make up such a far-fetched lie over some female who obviously doesn't want a bar of him. It doesn't make any sense. Pity Leah can't see that.'

Leah no longer knew what to think, for Alan was right in a way. It didn't make much sense. She didn't really believe Gerard was out to kidnap her. Violence was not his bag. He always used oral persuasion to get what he wanted. At worst, he appealed to an opponent's darker side to achieve his ends, playing up to their greed, or their love of power and position.

She couldn't see how pretending to be his twin brother could possibly persuade her back to her marriage. What could Gerard hope to achieve with a deception which could only be short-lived, at best? She would eventually find out the truth.

'Perhaps if I might make a suggestion?'

Leah whirled at the sound of the female voice, flushing as she realised the rest of the party had been standing around, witnessing—and possibly being entertained by—every embarrassing, humiliating word. Sandra was especially wide-eyed, obviously fascinated by the situation.

It was Peggy who had spoken, however. Geoff's wife. Once everyone'e eyes were upon her, she went on.

'I used to go to school with identical twins. They were the dead spit of each other, and liked to play awful jokes on everyone, swapping places all the time. But then one of them had an accident in the playground, running into another boy and chipping his front tooth. After that, we could always tell them apart. Perhaps, young man, you have some physical defect that your brother didn't have? That way this nice young lady could be sure. I can understand her reluctance to trust your word alone, if your brother is such a bad egg.'

Peggy's suggestion had clearly pole-axed him, his shoulders stiffening with instant tension.

Leah's stomach turned over when she saw that telltale muscle twitch along his jawline. Gerard did that all the time when put into an awkward or unpalatable position. His jaw muscle had twitched just like that when she'd told him she was bored that morning at breakfast, and also at a dinner party one night, when a Brisbane alderman had told him he would never pass a development Gerard had submitted to council.

That alderman had not been voted in at the upcoming election, when a sex scandal had erupted around him.

Her heart began to beat faster. So she'd been right all along. He *was* Gerard.

Everyone was staring at him now, staring and waiting. An electric tension filled the air.

'There must be *something*, man,' Alan grated out.

'There *is* a scar,' he said, startling Leah, since Gerard did not have a single flaw on his beautiful male body.

'But, frankly, it's a bit embarrassing to show, given its position. I'll give you a look, Alan, and you can tell Leah about it.'

CHAPTER THREE

'THAT'S not good enough!' was Leah's instant reaction, and everyone's eyes swung round to glare at her.

Their obvious exasperation with her ongoing attitude met with a defiantly lifting chin. 'Scars can be faked. I want to see it for myself. I think I have that right.'

Alan rolled his eyes, but the object of her scepticism merely shrugged. 'If you insist.'

'Geez, Leah,' Alan muttered. 'If it was anyone else...' He shook his head at her. 'All right. Take him below and set your stubborn mind at rest. But let that be an end to this bloody nonsense! Meanwhile, I'll get the old girl going. But don't be too long, madam. I want you up on deck once we're properly under way, complete with refreshment trays.'

His utter faith in Gareth's identity unnerved Leah. Was she making a complete fool of herself here?

Probably. But how could she blindly trust what this man was telling her? It had been her blind trust which had landed her in trouble in the first place. No! She had to see this scar for herself, and judge if it was real or not.

Her heart began thudding behind her ribs as she made her way along the deck towards the cabin. She didn't look over her shoulder to check if she was being followed. She could hear him right behind her. She could even *smell* him.

He smelt just like Gerard, she realised once they'd stepped into the confinement of the cabin. His body had that same scent which had always clung to Gerard's skin. Her husband used to shower morning and night, after which he'd spray this very expensive cologne over his body. It was called East Meets West, and had an exotic, musky fragrance.

Leah had grown to love that smell, had learnt to associate it with a naked Gerard sliding into the sheets beside her at night. It had primed her senses for what was to come without his having to say a word, or even touch her body. Every nerve-ending would be instantly on alert, clamouring for release.

No way could she mistake that scent for another. The odds of Gerard's long-lost twin using the same exclusive and expensive cologne were so remote as to be not worth considering.

This new situation threw Leah totally, because despite her other doubts she'd been half convinced by Alan's logical arguments. But the cologne was much more conclusive evidence than a twitching jaw muscle. *That* could have been put down to similar body language. Her own brothers had some identical physical habits and they weren't even identical twins.

But this…this could not be explained away so easily, neither could her ongoing physical reaction to the man. Why, even now, without looking at him, she felt her skin prickling, the hairs on the back of her neck standing on end. It wasn't just his scent. It was his whole being. His sexual aura.

She could feel her own flesh, that finely tuned Gerard-programmed flesh, responding as it always had when he was near. Her pulse-rate picked up its beat. Her skin temperature rose. Her nipples hardened.

To have him witness this unwilling arousal would be the highest of humiliations! Shame forced her to pull herself together, then to turn and try to face him with apparent composure.

Leah experienced a deep satisfaction in her surprising ability to appear in total control. Gerard wasn't the only one who could pretend, she realised.

It was to be thanked, however, that her colourful shorts and T-shirt were of the modern baggy variety. Anything clinging would have been a disaster.

'Well?' she said coolly. 'Let's see this scar. Or are you going to admit now, Gerard, that there isn't one?'

He frowned at her for a moment, before lifting his hands abruptly to the waistband of his shorts. When he pulled open the securing stud and shot down the zipper, Leah gulped.

Just who was calling whose bluff here?

'Don't say I didn't warn you,' he said.

Leah's throat thickened when he dropped his shorts to his ankles, lifted his T-shirt, then yanked the narrow band of his white underpants downwards.

Her gasp reverberated with shock. But not the shock she'd been fearing. He didn't expose himself. Not quite. What he did expose, however, was the largest, nastiest scar she'd ever seen. It zig-zagged its ugly way from his right hip down across his lower abdomen, ending in his groin: a lightning-strike of stark horror against his deeply tanned skin.

It was obviously not faked, or new. New scars were red, or pink, or even purple. Not white.

Gareth was also tanned all over. Gerard had never had the time for such frivolities as an all-over tan.

'Touch it,' he ordered curtly. 'I think you'll find it's real enough.'

Leah shrank from doing any such thing.

'Go on,' he insisted. 'I want you to be sure.'

Leah swallowed before reaching out with a tentative trembling hand. It wasn't revulsion which made her hesitant, but a fear of touching him. Anywhere.

Suddenly it wasn't the scar which was drawing her eyes but the rest of him, especially that which was being ineffectually contained by his briefs. Clearly he was an impressively equipped man, as impressive as his brother. But of course he would be, wouldn't he? They were identical twins.

Leah's gaze skittered back to the scar, her fingertip quivering as it made tentative contact with the puckered skin. When he flinched at her touch her hand immediately dropped away, her eyes jerking up to his.

'H…how did it happen?' she asked, appalled by her breathless state, plus the wild hammering of her heart.

'A car accident some time back,' came the curt reply. He bent abruptly and dragged his shorts back up to his waist. 'A truck smashed into me at an intersection.'

Leah struggled with her feelings. Clearly the man standing before her *wasn't* Gerard, yet he could still stir her sexually. Which said what of her feelings for her husband? Not much except that they must be very superficial, and shallow. Easily transferred from one twin to another.

She shook her head in confusion. That didn't feel right, didn't feel right at all. She'd loved Gerard. She still loved him. She was sure of it.

'You still don't believe me?'

She frowned up at her husband's twin brother, and found excuses for his being able to turn her on. He *did* carry identical genes to Gerard, after all. When she looked at him, her brain automatically registered her husband's face and body. It didn't mean anything. It was simply an instinctive response which would fade in a few minutes.

'No, I *do* believe you. It's just hard, that's all. I had no idea Gerard had a brother, let alone a twin. I'm still a bit shell-shocked. You have no idea how much you look like him.'

'Oh, yes, I have,' he said ruefully as he snapped the waistband of his shorts shut and pulled his T-shirt back down. 'But looks are only skin-deep, Leah. Don't judge me on them.'

'I…I'll try not to,' she said, though she could not help feasting her eyes on his face and body. Slightly thinner than Gerard he might be, but he was still extremely attractive to her.

'That's good, because I'd like to speak to you further at some later date. I have to admit to being more than curious about you and my brother. For now, however, perhaps you'd better get back to doing your job before your boss loses his cool.'

All of a sudden the man himself popped his head through the cabin door, his long blond hair swinging around his bare shoulders. 'You two sorted everything out?'

'Perfectly,' Gareth answered for them both, in the same decisive way Gerard had when dealing with people.

Leah groaned silently. She supposed there were going to be a lot of disturbing similarities about the two brothers. She was as curious about Gareth as he was about her, but the thought of spending more time with him sent her into a spin.

'In that case, shake a leg with the food and drinks, Leah,' Alan advised brusquely. 'Perhaps Gareth can help you.'

'Yes, I'd like that,' he agreed, before Leah could say a word. 'As long as my newly found sister-in-law doesn't mind,' he added, a sudden smile quite blowing Leah away. Smiling, he was as devastatingly handsome and charming as Gerard had been.

'She won't, if she knows what's good for her,' Alan grated out before abruptly disappearing.

'You don't mind, do you?' Gareth asked, his eyes searching hers.

'No. Not really. It's just that...'

'That what?'

That I can't look at you without wanting to touch you again, came the awful secret admission. *Without wanting you...*

Leah tried to keep the shock from showing on her face.

It was only natural, she reasoned in desperation. He looked so much like Gerard. Smelt like him. Spoke like him. It was perfectly but perversely natural that her body, long starved of sexual satisfaction, would crave it from this man who so resembled the man she loved.

But, dear God, it was difficult to cope with.

'I...I get upset when I look at you,' she said quite truthfully.

His blue eyes clouded. 'You hate Gerard that much?'

'Yes,' she said. It was the truth too. She loved him *and* hated him.

'I see,' he said thoughtfully. 'I'm sorry. The last thing I want is to upset you. But, other than my jumping overboard, I'm afraid you're condemned to look at me occasionally. Under those circumstances, it's better I help you serve, don't you think? That way I'll be standing beside you and not in front of you.'

She shook her head, a small wry smile playing on her lips. 'I see you and your brother are more alike than in looks alone. You both have the gift of the gab. Gerard could talk his way out of the gallows, if needs be.'

Gareth's smile was equally wry. 'They don't hang people in Australia these days, though I suppose if they did, you wouldn't object to Gerard meeting his maker that way.'

'Hanging's too good for him,' Leah said bitterly. 'But let's not talk about Gerard. We have work to do. This way.' She whirled and walked over to the two narrow wooden steps which led down to the galley.

'Watch your head!' she threw over her shoulder as an afterthought, just as Gareth's forehead made contact with the overhead beam.

The sympathetic female in Leah responded to the sickening clunk, and before she could think better of it she'd swung round to offer succour and comfort, her soft hands finding the hard wall of his chest.

'Are...are you all right?' she asked shakily, her eyes lifting to his.

'I guess I'll survive.' He stopped rubbing the reddening lump to look down, first at where she was touching him, then deep into her eyes.

She should have stepped back straight away. She realised that afterwards. But she didn't. She stayed right where she was, her palms flat against his solid warmth, her wide-eyed gaze wallowing in his.

How many moments passed with their standing there like that? Leah had no idea. In hindsight, it felt like an eternity, but it was probably only a couple of seconds before he took hold of her trespassing hands and lifted them away from his flesh.

'Some ice might be a good idea,' he said.

His disposing of her hands plus his crushingly matter-of-fact tone shot her back to reality in a rush.

'Yes, yes, of course,' she said, embarrassment making her clumsy as she whirled away from him and knocked into the nearest bench, rattling the tray of clean but empty glasses which lay in waiting to be filled. Her muttered swear-word was less than lady-like. Her hands shot out to clasp the edge of the darned thing in an attempt to steady the glasses, and her own stupidly racing heart.

'Forget the ice,' Gareth said sharply from where he was standing just behind her. 'I'm fine. Truly. Look, I think I'd better go up on deck with the others and leave you to do this alone. I can see my presence upsets you. I'll tell Alan I was getting in your way and that you'll be making an appearance shortly.'

She spun round to protest, but he was already on his way, ducking his head as he took the steps two at a time and disappeared from sight.

It was just as well, she realised after her initial dismay. He *did* upset her, though not perhaps as he imagined he did. He could never understand what just looking at him did to her, let alone touching him. When her hands had lain against his beating heart she'd been overwhelmed with a deep inner yearning to lay her head there, as she had done with Gerard a thousand times.

Oh, how safe she'd once felt in her husband's arms. And how loved. She would have given anything to feel that again, had been impelled, for one mad glorious moment, to recapture the experience with Gareth, by closing her eyes and pretending he was Gerard.

It would have been so easy.

Or would it?

Gareth had given no indication he would have tolerated her doing any such thing. Just the opposite, in fact.

Not by look or action did he show any attraction towards her. Just because *she* was unconsciously attracted to his husband's twin it didn't mean the reverse held true, although she *had* read somewhere that identical twins tended to be drawn to the same physical types. There had been cases of such twins, separated at birth, who, when they were reunited as adults, found they had chosen similar professions, hobbies *and* wives.

Gareth, however, showed no such inclination. Leah knew when a man fancied her. It was in their eyes, and their actions. She'd had plenty of experience in the last six months, recognising the signs and warding off a lot of unwanted passes.

Her marriage to Gerard had changed her somehow when it came to her ability to attract the opposite sex. Where before she'd had the occasional admirer, men now went after her in droves. She wasn't sure why. She didn't think she looked any different. And she certainly made no attempts to attract their attention with her appearance. No make-up was the order of the day. Her hair was worn long and straight. Her clothing mostly consisted of jeans or shorts, and loose tops. Yet still she had to tolerate male ogling and constant come-ons.

It seemed her brother-in-law, however, was not going to represent a problem in that department.

Which was a relief to Leah, now that she was over that one mad impulse. God, yes! Imagine what might have happened if Gareth *had* fancied her. She would have been put in a terrible position, trying to resist what she realised could only be an illusion.

For it wasn't Gareth she was actually responding to, was it? It was Gerard. His memory. His influence. His power, which was more far-reaching than even Leah could ever have imagined, coming to her clear across the country in the guise of another man.

Yes, it was to be thanked that Gareth didn't fancy her. For heaven alone knew what might happen if he did!

CHAPTER FOUR

ALAN charged a few more dollars per person than the other sunset cruises available, but supplied champagne, orange juice and soft drink, whereas the other operators asked people to bring their own drinks. Not a good idea when they had to carry them.

Taking a deep breath, Leah picked up the tray of drinks and carried it carefully out on deck. She turned automatically towards the back of the boat where everyone usually grouped, possibly because there was more room, but mostly because that was where Alan stood at the wheel, answering their questions and generally entertaining all and sundry with tales of the old pearling days.

'Yep,' he was saying as she approached, 'thousands of young Japanese divers died from the bends back then. But that didn't stop more from coming, seeking quick riches. Ah, here's Leah with some bubbly. I'll bet back in the old days the crew of *The Zephyr* would have liked to be served by such a pretty maid at the end of the day, don't you think, Gareth?'

Gareth, who'd been sitting a little aside from the others and staring out at the horizon, glanced around. 'Assuredly. You're a lucky man, Alan, to be surrounded by such beauty on a daily basis,' he said, and while his hand waved out to where the sun was sinking low in the sky and casting its golden glow over the water his eyes were looking straight at Leah.

Leah was taken aback, then quite flustered, worried now that she might have been mistaken in her earlier assessment about Gareth not finding her attractive. Yet it wasn't anything like lust she saw in his eyes. It was something else. But what? Concern? Curiosity? Surely not caring. How could he care about her when he'd only just met her?

She tried not to colour under his regard, thankful for the sea breeze which was helping cool her suddenly hot skin.

'You won't find sunsets anywhere in Australia to match these,' Alan was saying. 'Darwin tries to lay claim to better, but they don't compare in my opinion. No sunset here is the same, I've found. It changes every night with the various cloud covers. I never get tired of them.'

Leah finally managed to break away from Gareth's strangely hypnotic gaze and offer the tray around. By the time she got to Gareth she imagined she was totally under control again, only to have that illusion shattered the moment he spoke.

'When can we meet privately?' he said, his eyes meeting hers. Damn, but she wished he didn't have Gerard's eyes, even if they did hold a much softer expression.

'Well I…I don't know exactly…'

'Tonight, after the cruise?' he suggested while she waffled.

The imminency and potential intimacy of such a

meeting brought panic. 'No, no I can't make it to-night,' she said swiftly, though of course she could.

'Why not?' he asked as he took one of the glasses of soft drink.

Gerard would have taken the champagne, came Leah's automatic thought. He liked champagne. He liked all things expensive. He liked to work hard, drink hard, play hard. There were no soft options for Gareth's brother. No soft anything.

His brother, she conceded, was a different style of man entirely. More relaxed. Less driven. Yet for all that still very, very attractive to her.

For the first time she wondered what Gerard would do if he found out she'd met up with his estranged twin brother. Just thinking about such a possibility turned her stomach. Gerard had been very possessive of her. And quite jealous at times. He'd hated other men admiring her, or looking at her too much. She just knew he would hate her having anything to do with Gareth.

'I'm busy tonight,' she said briskly. 'How about lunchtime tomorrow? I could meet you in Broome somewhere.' Lunch was much better. And much safer. Daylight, as opposed to night-time.

Leah feared meeting Gareth at night. Night-time was for lovers…

'Very well. Name the time and the place.'

'Where are you staying?'

'The Roebuck Bay apartments.'

Not far from her place, actually. She could walk there, no trouble.

'I know where they are,' she said. 'I'll meet you

outside Reception at noon. We can walk down town from there.'

'I have a hire car.'

'Whatever. Now I must go get the food, or Alan'll give me the sack.'

'I doubt it,' she heard Gareth mutter as she walked away.

Leah frowned over the dry remark as she made her way back to the galley. Did Gareth think she and Alan were some kind of item? It wouldn't be the first time, she supposed. Several people already presumed they were sleeping together, especially when she didn't go home to her rented room after the cruise, but stayed aboard the lugger for the night.

Little did those people know they were the nights Alan picked up some wealthy widow who didn't fancy a night rolling around in Alan's cramped cabin. Invariably such women invited him back to their own more luxurious tourist accommodation, usually at the nearby Cable Beach Resort. On those occasions Alan would offer Leah a bonus to stay aboard and mind the ship, which she quite happily did. It was lovely to lie out on the deck under the moonlight, sipping the left over champagne and watching the stars twinkle against the black canvas of a clear night sky.

When the three girls she shared a house with in Broome made pointed remarks about herself and Alan Leah didn't bother to deny it. It suited her to let them think she had a boyfriend of sorts. It gave her some sort of protection from all the men which trailed through the place ad infinitum. Her housemates were good-time girls—working in Broome for the tourist season—and the old house they shared rocked to wild parties every weekend.

It bothered Leah momentarily that Gareth might think she and Alan were lovers. Till she quickly reasoned that such a situation might be all for the best as well. The last thing she needed was to complicate things with Gerard's twin brother. Hadn't she made enough of a mess of her life so far? She would meet Gareth for one simple lunch, answer his questions, ask a few of her own, then have nothing more to do with him!

Exhaling a deep, shuddering breath, Leah took the food out of the fridge and placed it on the bench before peeling off the plastic wraps. She picked up the first plate and balanced it on her left hand. It was wide and round and held a selection of crackers covered with various seafood delicacies. She then picked up the second server, which catered for people with simpler tastes. Carrot and celery sticks, a dip, cheese and salami.

The sun was near to setting when she emerged back on deck, its golden hue having deepened to that wonderfully rich orange. It would deepen even further shortly, sometimes going blood-red before sinking down behind the horizon. Alan was right. You never tired of watching the sunsets over Cable Beach.

The two inseparable couples had gravitated towards the western side of the boat to get the best view, she noted. Sandra, however, clung to Alan's side, gushing and gammering. Sunsets had no interest for women like her.

Gareth had wandered right up to the front of the

boat and was leaning against the railing, looking remote and mysterious. Which he was, in a way. Where had he come from? Leah wondered. What did he do for a living? Why was he here, in this far corner of Australia?

Fate had indeed been fickle to bring Gerard's identical twin to the small spot his ex-wife had chosen as sanctuary.

If Leah was honest, there was a lingering doubt in her mind over this last strange coincidence. Okay, she finally believed he wasn't Gerard, but there was still something about all this that bothered her greatly, aside from the unfortunate fact he reminded her so much of her husband.

Leah plied everyone down at the back of the boat with food before making her way reluctantly forward, by which time she was awfully tense.

Gareth didn't seem to notice her approach. He'd stopped looking at the sunset and was leaning right over the railing and peering intently down to where the bow of the boat was cleaving through the water. There was quite a breeze up and the old lugger was really moving along, not like the previous evening, when they had been so becalmed Alan had had to start the engine.

Leah frowned as her gaze moved almost hungrily over his body, down his back to his buttocks, trim and taut beneath his hip-hugging shorts. She knew exactly how his buttocks would look naked. How they would feel.

Her fingers tightened around the plates as she

thought of the many times her nails had dug into
Gerard's buttocks as she'd climaxed beneath him.

'Something to eat, Gareth?' she managed to ask
through suddenly dry lips.

'Dolphins,' he said by way of an answer, and continued to stare downwards, clearly entranced by the
sight of several of the beautiful creatures skimming
sleekly through the water.

She rather admired his obvious and almost childlike
pleasure. Watching dolphins was the kind of simple
activity Gerard would have scorned as a waste of
time.

'They often follow the boat,' she said. 'Especially
when we get some speed up. It's a game, I think,
keeping up and even leaping across the bow with
inches to spare.'

'A bit like a car racing a train,' he said, and glanced
up, his face quite flushed with excitement. Or perhaps
it was the light of the sunset on his olive skin.
Whatever, it looked wonderful on him.

She had to look away, afraid again of the feelings
coursing through her. How could she want him like
this? It felt like a betrayal of her love for his brother.

Once she had herself under control again, her eyes
moved slowly back to face him, a plastic smile on her
mouth. 'Are you a seafood man, or a cheese and dip
man?' she asked as she held both trays out for his
perusal.

'Don't you know?' he smiled.

She just stared at him.

'My brother and I have similar tastes,' he elabo-
rated as he selected one of the crab-topped crackers.

'In just about everything actually,' he added, then popped the cracker into his mouth.

Leah's eyes flew to his till she realised he wasn't coming on to her, simply stating a fact. If he'd been referring to his taste in women—specifically *her*—then it certainly didn't show in his face, which remained totally devoid of anything smacking of desire.

Leah's relief wasn't total, however. She seemed to have enough desire for both of them. How her heart had leapt in that second when she'd thought he fancied her. It was clear she'd be in deep, deep trouble if Gareth ever made a pass at her. How could she resist him? She'd never been able to resist his brother. And he was his brother's mirror image.

She just stood there for a moment, her head and stomach whirling.

'Is something wrong, Leah?' Gareth asked gently.

'No, no, not at all,' she denied, finding a breezy smile from somewhere. 'I was just thinking. But I'd better get back to the others. Here. Take another cracker before I go.'

He did, and she hurried back to Alan and co.

The boat had turned and was cruising back to their starting point by the time Gareth rejoined the rest of the party. Alan was regaling everyone with another of his horror stories of the old days, this time about a cyclone which had devastated the pearling fleet and practically flattened Broome. Leah had just emerged from the cabin with fresh drinks and was standing not far from Alan, shaking her head at his somewhat exaggerated story-telling.

'But not to worry, folks,' he finished up. 'Whilst

Broome still has its share of cyclones, we don't get any at this time of year. Except for madam, here,' he added teasingly, nodding towards Leah. 'She really kicked up a storm for a while there with you, Gareth, didn't she? Still, that brother of yours must be a right royal rotter if Leah here couldn't stomach him. She's a real sweetie, aren't you darlin'?' he said, and reached out to curl an arm round her waist, drawing her to his side.

Leah tried not to look too startled, or spill the remaining drinks, because she had a good idea what was going on. Sandra had proved too much, even for Alan, and he wanted an out. It wasn't the first time he'd subtly—and this time not so subtly—used Leah to deflect a female. From the silky pout on Sandra's scarlet-glossed lips, his message was getting through.

Leah slid her eyes in Gareth's direction to see what *he* thought of the situation.

His expression was totally unreadable, but his knuckles showed white where his hand gripped the bulkhead.

'Perhaps I should warn you,' came his dry remark, 'that my brother would not take too kindly to any man who dared put a hand on his wife.'

Alan laughed. 'Really? Then it's just as well he's not here, isn't it?' he said, tightening his hold on Leah's waist, then bending to kiss her on the cheek.

Leah decided enough was enough, wriggling out of Alan's embrace and throwing him a reproachful glance. 'I wouldn't make jokes about my husband, Alan. He's is a very rich, very powerful and very ruthless man.'

'Not over here, he isn't,' Alan scoffed.

'I wouldn't be too sure about that,' Leah muttered, unease returning at this discussion about Gerard. Money, she knew, had few boundaries and many leverages.

'He's certainly not a man to be underestimated,' Gareth warned, his eyes on Leah, not Alan.

Her chin shot up. 'I don't underestimate him, believe me. Why do you think I'm here, hiding?'

Gareth frowned. 'Are you saying you're afraid of him?'

'He's not a man to be crossed.'

'Gerard might be many things, but he would never be violent. Never!'

Although she agreed with him on that score, Leah was still irritated by Gareth's vehement defence of her brother. 'You sound very sure of that. Yet how many years is it since you've seen him, or spoken to him?'

'We parted company when we were twenty-three. But I've followed his career closely ever since. Admittedly, he does have a ruthless streak with his business enemies, but he confines his attacks to the verbal, never the physical. And I gather he *has* done some good with his money over the years. Gives a lot of charities.'

'Huh!' Leah scorned. 'Don't believe everything you read in the newspapers. Gerard is a clever manipulator of the media. Fact is, he's a clever manipulator all round,' she added bitterly. 'But I'm sure everyone here doesn't want their evening spoilt with talk of my clever conman of a husband. Now, does anyone else want another drink?'

Leah busied herself with the hostessing part of her job for the next ten minutes before excusing herself and escaping down below. Once there, she started washing up, sighing repeatedly in an effort to relax the tension between her shoulders.

Still, it was a relief to be away from Gareth's probing eyes. He really had no idea about the man Gerard was these days. She doubted he fully understood the extent of his brother's cold-blooded ways. Neither could he ever appreciate why she was so afraid of him.

Leah didn't dare tell him the truth: that Gerard's sexual power over her was so strong it carried the risk of total corruption to his will, so strong that his identical twin could tap into that wicked power if he ever wanted to.

Leah shuddered at the thought.

'Alan said you'd point me to the bathroom.'

Leah spun round from the sink to find Gareth less than a metre behind her. How long had he been standing there? Had he been watching her, listening to her moan and groan?

His physical presence in the cramped galley unnerved her unbearably. Then there was that tantalising scent wafting from his skin again, plus an even more overpowering awareness of his very male body. She hated looking up into his handsome face and seeing Gerard looking back at her.

'It's down there,' she said curtly, pointing towards some narrow ladder-like steps in the far corner. 'The second door on the left. Not the first one. That's

Alan's cabin. You'll have to watch your head again. And your step.'

'Right.' She watched him go, ducking his head and moving carefully.

She contemplated fleeing before his return but decided that was silly, so she returned to the washing up and had actually finished it by the time he reappeared, looking pale and drawn. Leah was so used to boats that it rarely occurred to her that anyone might get seasick. She'd thought he simply wanted to use the toilet.

'Goodness, you don't look at all well,' she said, moved to sympathy by his wretched expression. 'But not to worry. You'll be off the boat in a few minutes.'

He stared hard at her as though he didn't know what she was talking about. But then he seemed to regather his wits. 'I'm all right,' he said brusquely, though he didn't look it. 'Look, if you don't want to meet me tomorrow then just say so.'

She was taken aback by his abruptness, till she conceded it was probably because he wasn't feeling well.

'It's not that I don't *want* to, Gareth,' she said. 'It's just that…that…'

'That what, for pity's sake?' he snapped. 'You want to keep on hiding indefinitely, do you? Or is it that you've found yourself a new life on this boat with Alan and you don't want to even talk or think about the fact you have a husband back in Brisbane who's probably worried sick about you?'

'The only thing Gerard would be worried about,' she snapped back, 'is his precious ego! And why are you defending him? You haven't had anything to do with him for ten years. A brother doesn't cut his twin out of his life like that without good cause. What did he do to you, Gareth? Cheat you out of an inheritance? Blame you for something *he* did? Sleep with your girlfriend?'

Gareth stared at her for several tense seconds. And then his shoulders sagged.

'I had no idea,' he said wearily.

'No idea about what?'

His eyes lifted and they were incredibly sad. 'That Gerard would hurt anyone as much as he obviously hurt you. I'm so sorry, Leah. Believe it or not, he was a pretty good bloke once. I rather admired him. We came to a parting of the ways after Dad died. He blamed our mother, you see. And it changed him dramatically.'

'Don't keep defending him,' she groaned. 'There *is* no defence. I don't want to *hear* any defence. You have no idea what he did to me. He lied to me, told me he loved me and married me under false pretences. He played me for a fool, taking all the love I had to give and giving me nothing in return but lies. I was no more to him than another land acquisition, to be developed and made over to his requirements. I wasn't a human being with feelings. I was a possession, a…a project!'

He nodded. 'You're right. There is no defence for such behaviour. But still, don't you think you would have been better off staying and telling him where he'd gone wrong, asking for a divorce then and there?'

'I couldn't stay,' she rasped. 'You don't understand. I couldn't stay...' She hugged herself as she shuddered, her gaze dropping to the floor.

His finger under her chin was gentle, yet very, very male. With excruciating slowness he tipped her face upwards till their eyes met.

'You're right,' he said, bewilderment in his voice, 'I don't understand. If you weren't afraid of his hurting you in any way physically, then why run away? Why not face him with his shortcomings? That would seem the logical thing to do.'

Logic! When had logic anything to do with her responses to Gerard? From the moment he'd swept into her life she'd been under his spell.

Impossible to tell Gareth it had been herself she'd been afraid of, that pathetically weak creature who'd lain beneath her treacherous husband in mindless ecstasy even after finding out the awful truth about him, that pathetically weak creature who even now was so aroused by her husband's identical twin touching her that it was unbearable! Only a fingertip, yet it made her long for his arms to go around her, to pull her to him, kiss her, caress her, take her to that place where only Gerard could take her.

Or so she'd once imagined. Perverse it might be, but she knew Gareth could take her there too, for her body didn't seem to know the difference between the two men. Gerard... Gareth... They were the same in her eyes, *and* in her sexual responses to them.

She groaned with relief when Gareth's hand dropped away.

'What exactly are you hiding from, Leah?' he demanded to know, clearly puzzled. 'It has to be something you fear about Gerard. Tell me what it is.'

'I can't,' she said, hugging herself tightly in defence of her slowly disintegrating self.

'Why not?'

'You wouldn't understand. You don't know him like I do.'

'No,' he admitted, 'that's true. But I know him better than you realise. He's my other half.'

'He's wicked,' she whispered, and shut her eyes against the rush of memory. But in the darkness she could still feel his mouth covering hers, his hands caressing her breasts, his flesh fusing with hers.

She shuddered violently.

Her eyes flew open when Gareth started unpeeling her hands from where they were clasping her sides. 'No, don't!' she cried. 'Don't touch me. I don't want you to touch me.'

For a moment he looked as if she'd struck him.

'I'm sorry,' she said straight away. 'It's not you. Please understand that. When I react badly, it's not you.'

'All right. I'll try to remember that.'

'Look, I must go,' she told him abruptly. 'Alan will need me on deck to let down the sails.'

'Very well. But we're going to talk a lot more about this, Leah. Tomorrow...'

CHAPTER FIVE

THE temperature at eleven-thirty hovered around thirty degrees, as it did most days in Broome in June. The sea breezes wouldn't spring up till later in the afternoon.

Leah had been in a quandary all morning over what to wear for her lunch date with Gareth. Should she make an effort to look nice, or just throw on shorts and a T-shirt?

She'd calmed down somewhat overnight, well aware she'd overreacted to Gareth's sudden appearance in her life, and his appearance in general.

Of course she would find him physically attractive! He was the dead spit of the man she was mad about, who could reduce her to mush with a glance! But he wasn't Gerard and she just had to keep reminding herself of that. If she still felt twinges of desire when she looked at him today then that was only to be expected.

Thankfully, Gareth had shown no signs whatsoever of being smitten in any way with her. He hadn't leered or ogled, hadn't done a single darned thing to create any unease in her in a sexual sense.

In view of all these logical reasonings, Leah decided in the end not to dress *too* down for the occasion. Which meant she allowed herself a skirt and lipstick, instead of her usual baggy shorts and un-painted mouth.

The skirt was a floral wrap-around number, with a black background, which reached to mid-calf, the lip-stick a pink which matched most of the flowers.

She did run into some trouble selecting a top to go with the skirt.

In Broome, bras were out of the question most of the time. They were just too hot and too sticky. Leah had ended up with a heat rash when she'd persisted in wearing one during her first week there. Soon she'd joined the locals and thrown the darn things away. Her only underwear these days was a cotton G-string, which was considerably more than some girls wore.

She rarely gave her braless breasts a thought any more. But she did that morning.

Her breasts weren't big, but they were full and high, with pointy nipples. A black top would have been best. But she didn't have a black top. Black at-tracted the heat. No one wore black in Broome during the day.

She finally settled for a pink ribbed midriff top, which had a squashing effect on her bust but left her middle bare. Leah glared at it for a while, then shrugged philosophically. You couldn't have every-thing, and she supposed a bare middle was less pro-vocative than pokey-out nipples.

As she wound her long hair on top of her head in a haphazard self-tied knot she thought of the rather severe and sleekly glamorous hairstyle Gerard had steered her into soon after her marriage. Shoulder-length and always perfectly blow-dried, it had shone and swung like a sensual blonde curtain around her face, curving over her left eye and reaching down to her shoulders. Gerard had claimed that whenever she'd glanced up at him through her hair, especially across a crowded room or from the other side of a dinner table, she'd given him an instant erection.

She did not doubt it. He'd always been ready to make love to her at the end of an evening out, no matter how late they'd arrived home. He'd liked to undress her himself, slowly stripping her of the designer gowns he'd always chosen for her, gowns which sparkled and clung to her tall model-like figure.

He'd always left her jewellery on, however, she recalled now.

Had he gained some perverse pleasure in seeing her naked flesh decked in diamonds? In looking down at them while he reduced her to a moaning mindless creature, his own satisfaction increased by the mistaken belief that it was his wealth which had bought him the perfect puppet wife?

Gerard didn't know it, but she would have lived with him in a hovel. And been happy.

If only he'd loved her...

Leah sighed, then shook herself. This wasn't achieving anything, this maudlin thinking.

One day soon she'd be over Gerard, never to be tormented again by thoughts of 'what if' or 'what might have been'. But not today, she accepted with a weary sense of resignation. Today she had to meet with Gareth a second time and be reminded of her husband all over again.

Sighing, she slipped cheap silver hoops in her ears,

purchased at the local markets for two dollars—a far cry from the twenty-two-carat gold earrings which had once been a standard part of her everyday wear. Even so, her wearing even such simple jewellery would have brought comments from her ever curious housemates. Fortunately, they had day jobs, so she didn't have to put up with their questions about where she was going 'all dolled up'.

Finally, she was ready, a resurgence of nerves claiming her as she left the house and turned for the short walk down to the apartments where Gareth was staying.

There was curiosity along with the nerves, however. Gareth might want to ask her about her marriage to Gerard, but she had questions of her own.

The Roebuck Bay apartments were fairly new, overlooking the bay, a double-storeyed assortment of buildings, vaguely Mediterranean in style and colour. Stylish and spacious, they were frequented by tourists who liked comfort and room, plus the convenience of being able to cook themselves a meal.

It crossed Leah's mind as she walked up the road which ran alongside Roebuck Bay that Gareth couldn't be short of a bob if he was staying there. Still, she couldn't imagine Gerard's brother not being successful at whatever he did for a living.

Whatever that was...

Leah decided one of her first questions would be to ask him, along with what he was doing here in Broome, a coincidence which still niggled her a little.

A ten-minute stroll brought her to the circular driveway which led round to a door marked

'Reception'. There was an outdoor staircase to the left of this door which led up to the second-floor apartments. A long wooden seat rested against the wall to the right.

Leah settled on this seat to await Gareth's arrival. She was five minutes early, as was her usual habit. This had amused Gerard during their marriage. He had always been late. In hindsight, she saw this as another sign of his heartless arrogance; his lack of real caring of other people's feelings.

Gareth breezed down the outdoor staircase with two minutes to spare, looking coolly handsome in casual cream trousers and a brightly patterned short-sleeved shirt. Stylish sunglasses masked his eyes.

A blessing, Leah thought, in view of his other attractions. The thought also appealed that she could not see him looking at her in any way, either at her body or into her eyes.

She rose and smiled up at him.

'You're very punctual,' she said.

'So are you.'

'I only live just down the road.'

His forehead puckered into a frown. 'But I thought you lived on board the boat?'

'I do stay on board sometimes,' she said, quite truthfully, 'when Alan asks me to.'

'I see,' he said rather drily.

But he didn't at all, Leah conceded. He thought she and Alan were lovers. She'd let him think that the previous evening, had used the misconception in much the same way Alan had. An unnecessary precaution, really. The attraction and tension had all been on *her* side, not Gareth's.

Now, Leah gave the situation some more thought and accepted she didn't want Gareth go on believing she had moved into another man's bed so soon after her husband's, especially while she was still legally married to him. She'd condemned Gerard for his lies. She would not lie to his brother.

'Alan is not my lover,' she said bluntly. 'That little scenario out there on the deck last night was for Sandra's benefit.'

Gareth frowned his puzzlement. 'I don't understand.'

'Alan has this thing for older women,' she explained. 'He flirts with pretty well any single female over forty during the cruise. If she's reasonably attractive, that is. Unfortunately he sometimes finds out after a while that she's not quite his cup of tea.'

'So he uses you to put them off,' Gareth finished. 'That's not very above board, Leah,' he added, the beginnings of a smile on his mouth.

Leah appreciated his not making a big deal out of her misleading him, and shrugged lightly. 'He's the skipper. And he's really quite harmless. The older ladies love him. When he does click with someone, and wants to spend the night ashore with her, I stay on board and mind the boat.'

'I would have thought such ladies would enjoy a night with Alan on that romantic old tub.'

'A lot do.'

'But not you...?'

'No. Not with Alan, anyway. He's not my type at

all.' She couldn't help thinking how she would have loved spending a night on board *The Zephyr* with Gerard when they'd first been married and seemingly so in love. What a honeymoon spot it would have made, much better than the five-star hotels he'd taken her to all over the world. They could have lain together under the stars, soft breezes playing on their naked bodies, the gently rocking water a rhythmic backdrop to their lovemaking.

'With anyone else?' Gareth asked, speculation in his voice.

'Anyone else?' she repeated, her mind still fuzzy as it was jerked out of the lovely, yet distressing dream.

'Is there another man in your life now?' Gareth asked. 'Someone you spend romantic nights with?'

'No,' she said, her voice sharp.

'No one?' he persisted, scepticism in the question. 'In six months?'

'I doubt there'll be anyone in six years! I loved Gerard very much. He shattered me with his betrayal of that love.'

'You hate him now, don't you?'

She gritted her teeth. 'I *despise* him.'

'I see.'

'I doubt you do, Gareth,' she bit out. 'You know nothing of my marriage. Or me.'

'Then why don't you tell me all about both?' he said in a soothingly sympathetic voice. 'Come on.' He nodded his head across the road to where a smart grey four-wheel drive was parked under the shade of a tree. 'My chariot awaits. Let's go get ourselves a cool drink and some food. But I'll have to rely upon you to steer me somewhere where the food is decent. I don't know Broome too well yet. I only arrived yesterday.'

'And you came out on our cruise the very first night?' she asked as they crossed the road.

He shrugged his broad shoulders, then reached to open the passenger door for her. 'I didn't want to waste any time.'

Leah nodded and climbed up into the grey upholstered seat, automatically clicking on the seat-belt while he closed the door and strode around the front.

When he climbed in behind the wheel and shut the car door, Leah's nostrils were once again assailed by that sandalwood cologne, the one which reminded her so forcibly of Gerard. Every pore and nerve-ending in her body sprang to attention again. Another of those disquieting niggles about Gareth's true identity resurfaced.

This time she could not remain quiet.

'Gareth,' she said abruptly.

Her tone must have communicated something, for his head jerked up from where he'd been bending forwards slightly to start the engine. 'What?'

'I...that cologne you wear...'

He frowned. 'What about it?'

'It...it's the same one Gerard wears.'

All of a sudden she wished he wasn't wearing sunglasses. She would have liked to see the expression in his eyes.

He sank back slowly against the seat.

'What are you saying?' he said tautly. 'That you still think I might be Gerard?'

'I don't know what I'm saying.'

'Look, I've been using that same cologne for years. Obviously, so has Gerard. Why is that such a problem?'

'It's very expensive,' Leah pointed out.

'I'm well aware of that. Our mother gave us some on our twenty-first birthday and I guess we both got hooked. Once you get used to the best, it's hard to go back to the cheaper varieties. Still, if it bothers you, I'll stop using it.'

'Would you mind?'

'No. But it won't change the way I look, Leah. I'll still *look* the same as Gerard.'

'I realise that. But there's something about your smelling the same which I find...upsetting.'

She'd almost said arousing. Had very definitely thought it. She wasn't handling the familiar fragrance any better than she had the previous night.

'In that case I definitely won't wear it any more,' Gareth pronounced firmly. 'I'll buy some new stuff this very afternoon.'

She glanced across at him as he started the engine, feeling reassured about his identity once more but no less curious over Gareth, the man.

'I presume you're here in Broome on a holiday?' she asked.

'Uh-huh.'

'Why Broome?'

He shrugged. 'I was told it was a great place to get away from it all. I've been working too hard for too many years. I needed a break, and the time to reassess my life.'

So both brothers were workaholics, to a degree, Leah mused. But at least Gareth had realised it before it was too late.

'What is it you do, Gareth?'

'I'm an architect.'

Yes, that fitted, she thought. A creative and well-thought-of profession. Not as high profile or gung-ho as being a property developer, but Leah had no doubt that Gareth was a winner in his own field. He had that aura of confidence and decisiveness which went with success.

But he would be more of a quiet achiever, whereas Gerard wanted the world to know of *his* success. Both brothers built things. But Gareth would care about the style of building he created and the people who lived there. Gerard's focus had always been on the almighty dollar, she thought bitterly.

'Anything wrong with my being an architect?' he asked as he angled the car out onto the road and headed towards the centre of town.

'Not at all. I'm impressed. Do you work for a company, or have your own?'

'I have my own. I like to do things my way.'

She nodded. 'Yes. That's what I thought. You have that air about you.'

'What air?'

'The air of being a boss.'

'Ah...'

She wasn't sure if he was pleased by her saying that or not.

'Where is your company located?' she asked. 'Over here in Western Australia?'

'No. In Brisbane.'

'In Brisbane!' she exclaimed, shocked. 'You've been in Brisbane all this time!'

'Yes.'

Leah shook her head. 'I'll never understand Gerard. How on earth did he think he could keep you a secret indefinitely? Brisbane's not that big. Frankly, I don't understand why he kept you a secret at all!'

'The Gerard you married has no time for things past, Leah. I'm his past.'

Leah sighed. Gareth was so right. Gerard lived for the present, and for what he called 'progress'. He'd often said the past was not worth thinking about. He never countenanced regrets or recriminations. He always went forward. He was the most pragmatic man, not indulging in sentiment or sentimentality at all.

Except, of course, when it suited his purpose, she realised ruefully. He had not been above bringing her flowers, when he wanted to butter her up or smooth over something he might have done to upset her.

Not that he had transgressed often during the nine months of their seemingly idyllic marriage. A couple of times he'd left unexpectedly on business and had not telephoned till he was in the air and on his way. She'd been rather put out by his presumption that she wouldn't mind, that she would understand his business sometimes came first.

She'd tried to, but probably hadn't been able to keep the dismay out of her voice. Each time he'd come home with his arms filled with red roses and his pocket containing a very expensive piece of jewellery.

As a blushing and besotted new bride, she'd accepted his gestures in good faith, moved by his assertions that he'd missed her like mad and loved her even more after their separation. No matter how irritated or put-out she'd been while he was away, it had never taken him long to wind himself around her heart…and around her body.

Oh, how smugly sure of her he'd been! Give the silly little fool some flowers, and she'll melt in my arms.

The memory sickened her now.

'Penny for your thoughts?'

Leah's head whipped up to stare at Gareth, startling him with her wide-eyed look.

'What is it?' he said worriedly. 'What did I say?'

'That…that thing about a penny for my thoughts. That's what Gerard used to say to me. In just that way…'

'Did he?'

She continued to stare at him, her head spinning as she struggled to ease that sudden awful fear that this wasn't some long-lost twin brother sitting there but Gerard himself!

The furrows on his forehead deepened. 'Look, Leah, there's going to be lots of things about me that remind you of Gerard,' he said, reading her mind quite accurately. 'We're identical. I can't help that. But I'm not the man you married, Leah. I swear that to you on my mother's life.'

His mother's life. That was a pretty strong vow.

There was the scar too, don't forget, she reminded herself.

Leah sighed her relief. God, but she'd been really rattled there for a moment. Her stomach still felt squeamish.

'Which way?' Gareth asked, slowing as he approached an intersection.

'Turn right at the next street,' she directed him. 'Then second on the left. Park anywhere you can find a spot down that street.'

The town centre of Broome was pretty basic, consisting of two parallel streets lined by an array of small shops. A new air-conditioned supermarket *had* been built down in one far corner, and there *was* another larger shopping mall on the outskirts of town, but both had taken time to gain clientele, the locals not liking change.

And who could blame them? Leah thought as she glanced around her. Broome had its own character and very individual charm, a mixture of tropical remoteness and the Australian outback, with palm trees, red dirt and a simple architecture all of its own. No tall brick buildings in Broome. Nearly everything was made of wood, or corrugated iron, and hopefully cyclone-proof.

The developers were beginning to move in, however, seeing dollars signs with the increase in tourism. More land was being chopped up into housing blocks and more roads were being curbed and guttered. Leah could understand why the long-standing residents resented the changes. In twenty years' time Broome would be unrecognisable.

Progress, she decided, was not always in the interests of the community. Leah was glad now that Gerard's plans for Hidden Bay had fallen through. Her brothers were happy and content as they were. They didn't need to be successful and rich.

Successful and rich did not necessarily equate with happiness, she now appreciated.

'What a pretty little place Broome is,' Gareth remarked as he slid the Pajero into an angled spot under a convenient tree. 'Let's hope it stays that way. This do?' he asked, throwing his passenger a questioning glance.

They would have to walk a little way, but it would be nice to step back into a cool vehicle.

'Perfect,' Leah praised, and smiled at him.

'What's the smile for?'

'For being you,' she said.

'For being me?'

'Yes. For not looking around you and seeing nothing but developmental dollar signs.'

'Ah...Gerard again...'

The edge in his voice evoked guilt in Leah. 'I'm sorry. I don't mean to keep comparing you two.'

'It's quite all right,' he said. 'Compare all you like. From what I've heard so far, I'm confident I'll come out on top. Shall we go?'

She guided him to a small sidewalk café which wasn't flash but which served great fish and chips. And fantastic milkshakes.

Gareth smiled when she told him what she wanted.

'Order the same for me, then,' came his easygoing reply. 'I'm game. Here's twenty dollars. That should cover it.'

Leah left him sitting at one of the outdoor tables

while she went inside to order, thinking that this would never have happened with Gerard. For one thing, Gerard only ate at à la carte restaurants—even for lunch—and *he* always ordered. She'd once been very impressed with his knowledge of wine and food. He could order from a French menu like a native Parisian.

That type of thing no longer impressed her. It was shallow. Without any real value. The only qualities which impressed her in a man these days were honesty. And integrity.

She turned and glanced through the front window of the café at Gareth, happily stretched out in a white plastic chair, his handsome head shaded by a garishly striped beach umbrella.

Instinct told her Gareth had integrity. And honesty. On top of that, he had the same face and body which still enslaved her senses.

She stared at him and felt that tell-tale quickening once more.

What a shame she hadn't met him first...

'Here you are, miss,' the man behind the counter said at last. 'I've put it all on a tray for you.'

'Thanks.'

Gareth sat forward as she carried the tray towards the table, taking his sunglasses off as he did so.

Her step faltered when his gaze swept over her from her toes up. There was no denying the male admiration in his glittering blue eyes this time. They lingered momentarily on her bare midriff before lifting to the confined swell of her breasts beneath the tight pink top.

Panic ripped through Leah when she felt those

breasts prickle beneath his indisputably sexual scrutiny. She almost tripped on a rough bit of pavement when she started forward again, the malted milks rocking ominously from side to side.

'Got them!' Gareth said, jumping up and sweeping the silver containers into safe hands.

Leah laughed, though shakily. 'You almost had chocolate milk in your lap then.'

Without looking at him again, she balanced the tray on the edge of the table and set everything out quite efficiently and with no further mishap, swiftly unwrapping the cutlery which was wrapped in paper serviettes, putting out the salt, vinegar and sauce, before finally placing the plates of fish and chips between the knives and forks.

'You did that very well,' he complimented on sitting down in his place.

She handed him his change, then swung away to put the tray on a spare table.

'I've had plenty of practice with serving up food.' She sat down and shook out her serviette. 'Aside from my more recent activities, I was the chief cook and bottlewasher for my brothers for years.'

'You must tell me about your life, Leah. *Before* you met Gerard,' he added drily.

She did, happy to find distraction from the panic she'd been trying to damp down since Gareth had looked at her the way he had. But dear heaven…

'Do you regret leaving Hidden Bay?' he asked when she'd finished telling him her life story, right up to her marriage.

'Every day.'

'Why didn't you go back there after you left Gerard?'

'I couldn't. Gerard would have found me.'

Gareth frowned. 'This is the part I don't understand, Leah.'

'No,' she said grimly. 'And I doubt you ever will. So don't ask me about it!'

He opened his mouth, then closed it again in a reluctant acceptance of her stance. 'Let's move on to your marriage. Were you happy to begin with?'

'Very happy. I thought Gerard loved me. I was prepared to make sacrifices for that love.'

'Sacrifices?' he asked in puzzled tones. 'What kind of sacrifices? You would have had everything a woman desired, surely.'

Leah could only shake her head at him. 'Spoken like a man. Do you honestly think that all a woman wants from a marriage is material things?'

'I would have thought they'd go a long way.'

'Then you'd be wrong. Oh, I won't deny a woman likes a certain degree of security, but that's more for the children she hopes to have. I gave up a lot to marry Gerard, more than I should have. I missed my life at Hidden Bay terribly. Missed the boat. Missed the sea. Missed my brothers.

'Frankly, I'm not sure that even if I hadn't overheard Gerard saying those dreadful things I would have stayed happy with him. He never took the time to talk to me about his work, or to understand me. He brushed aside my very real complaint that I needed something worthwhile to do during the day, suggesting instead that I take a silly cooking course. What would I do with that, I ask you? He employed a cook who refused to let me in the kitchen door!'

'There are a lot of women who would envy that lifestyle, Leah,' Gareth pointed out.

'Then it's a pity Gerard didn't marry one!' she snapped.

'Perhaps he wanted you.'

'Yes, of course he wanted me. He thought I was the perfect patsy. The perfect fool. I believed everything he told me.'

'Are you sure everything he said to you was a lie?'

'Of course I'm sure. I heard him say so as clear as a bell. He didn't love me. He'd never loved me. Yet he told me so every day, would whisper it when we made love,' she went on in strangled tones. 'Especially when he…when I…'

Her voice broke before she could make the humiliating confession: that her husband had told her he loved her even as she came, beneath him.

Gareth looked appalled.

'I…I don't want to talk about him any more,' she choked out raggedly, her eyes shifting from Gareth's shocked face to stare glazedly down the street.

Gradually her eyes focused on the people wandering up and down the pavement, her attention drawn to a well-dressed man with a mobile phone to his ear, not too common a sight in Broome. Leah frowned as she realised he was vaguely familiar. The man turned momentarily to face her direction and she sucked in a sharp breath.

'My God!' she gasped aloud. 'Nigel!'

CHAPTER SIX

'WHO?' Gareth asked, peering down the street.

But Nigel had disappeared.

Leah found she was shaking. Her fork clattered onto the near empty plate. 'It was Nigel,' she choked out. 'Gerard's personal pilot. He…he was watching me. I'm sure of it. Watching *us*!'

'What?' Gareth was on his feet. 'Where? Show me!'

'He's gone.'

'He can't have gone far. Do you want to go after him? I'll go with you.'

'God, no.'

'Why not?'

She just shuddered. She felt ill.

'Leah, for pity's sake, stop this,' Gareth said firmly. 'He's just a man.'

'Who?' she said bitterly. 'Nigel? Or Gerard?'

'Both. Now are you absolutely sure it *was* this Nigel person?'

Was she? She'd only seen him for a couple of seconds. Nigel wasn't so distinctive a man. He was very average. He looked like a lot of other men, actually. Not tall. Not dark. Not handsome.

'No,' she said wearily at last. 'I guess I'm not absolutely sure.'

'If Gerard were here in Broome, then he'd contact you, wouldn't he?'

'Oh, yes.' Gerard was no coward. Not like his wife.

'Then that settles it. He's not here. You must have been mistaken about this Nigel person. Understandable, given your obvious state of mind. You're very jumpy, Leah. I suppose I'm to blame for that.'

'I'm a bit mixed up, that's for sure,' she said raggedly.

Gareth reached over the table and picked up her hand. 'You have to move on, Leah,' he said softly as he stroked the back of her hand with gentle fingertips. 'You have to forget Gerard.'

She didn't react too badly to his touch this time, accepting his tactile comfort without panicking, or being swamped with dark desires. She was too distraught for such tempestuous feelings. Seeing Nigel—or thinking she had—had left her feeling disorientated, and very vulnerable.

Her eyes lifted to Gareth's and for once she didn't see Gerard, but a man with a face full of concern and caring.

'I'd like to forget him,' she said unhappily. 'Believe me.'

'You need to find someone new,' he said, his eyes holding hers. 'Someone to love and who'll truly love you in return. You must put aside the past and get on with your life, Leah. No more hiding. No more running away. Stop looking back and go forward.'

'That's easier said than done. I don't even know where to start.'

'I'll tell you where. The next time a man asks you out, if you like him at all, you should say yes.'

He stared at her for several long and incredibly meaningful moments, and Leah found herself holding her breath, waiting for him to say what she suddenly feared he was going to say.

And then he said it.

'Come out with *me*, Leah.'

Now she snatched her hand away, her eyes rounding even while her heart galloped.

'I liked you the first moment I saw you,' he said. '*More* than liked.'

'No!' she protested, shaking her head violently at him. He had no idea what he was saying. And asking.

'Oh, yes. Very much so.'

'But I…I can't go out with *you*!'

'Why not? I promise you I'm not two-timing anyone. I'm here alone, and I have no wife or girlfriend hidden at home in Brisbane who would object. All you have to do is say yes.'

She jumped to her feet, unable to stay calmly sitting there. She hurried across the street away from him, but he soon fell into step beside her.

'You can't run away from everything, Leah,' he ground out. 'You're as attracted to me as I am to you. I *know* you are.'

'You don't know what you're saying! I'm your brother's wife!'

'In name only. You told me yourself. You despise him. You left him.'

She found herself automatically heading back to where Gareth had parked the Pajero, the shops and the tourists quickly left behind. The pavement they were striding along was quite deserted.

'I haven't divorced him yet,' she threw over her shoulder.

'You will, though. *Won't* you?'

'I... I...'

He grabbed her arm and spun her round, his face harder than she'd ever seen it. 'What are you trying to say? That you're still in love with him?'

'I don't know.' She kept shaking her head in an agony of confusion. 'Dear God, I don't know anything any more!'

Suddenly she burst into tears, burying her face in her hands. She had no strength to stop him from taking her in his arms and cradling her against him.

'Oh, you poor darling,' he crooned as he held her close. 'You poor, poor darling...'

She sobbed into his shirt, her agony and confusion increasing with the feelings which erupted within her as he stroked her hair and back. They were stronger than what she'd felt the previous night, equally as strong as anything she'd felt with Gerard. Before she knew it she was sliding her arms around Gareth's waist, clinging to him, wanting him with a want which was beyond wanting.

His instant tension communicated itself to her in his frozen hands. But there was a part of him which wasn't frozen, which was hot and throbbingly alive, pressing its insistently hard length into the soft swell of her stomach. She imagined it complementing her own empty, craven flesh, filling it as only Gerard— or Gerard's twin—could fill it.

The temptation to just surrender to the moment in all its wild madness was acute. But she just couldn't do it. She wasn't like Gerard. She would not use people. Gareth was a decent man. He deserved better than a mixed-up fool who didn't know which brother it was she was wanting.

With the last vestiges of her will she wrenched herself out of his arms and began to run, not looking back.

She ran till she could not take another step. She was bent over, gasping for breath, when the Pajero slid to a stop beside her.

'Get in,' he ordered firmly, leaning over to push open the passenger door.

She straightened with a groan, her chest still rising and falling. Her hair had half fallen down with her flight, long sun-kissed strands hanging around her flushed face.

The man behind the wheel tightened his grip as he stared at her. He thought she was the most beautiful thing he'd ever seen, and he wanted her so much he ached unbearably.

But he could see he would have to go carefully to win what he wanted even more than her lovely body. He wanted *her, his, for ever*!

Leah's shoulders sagged as she finally gave in to common sense. Running away *was* futile. It achieved nothing. She'd run away from Gerard, and six months later she was still running.

It was time to stop. Even she could see that.

She walked over and climbed up into the car, pulling the door shut after her and collapsing back against the seat with a shuddering sigh.

Gareth negotiated a U-turn before angling the car over to the side of the road and snapping off the engine.

'Now, let's be strictly honest with each other,' he started, with a dark intensity in his voice. 'What happened back there betrayed you *do* feel attracted to me in return. Do you deny that?'

How could she? Her sigh was a mixture of distress and defeat. 'I'm not in a position to deny or confirm it, Gareth, because frankly I don't know who it is I'm attracted to. That's why I get so upset when you're around. When I look at you I see Gerard. Maybe what I feel for you is really for my husband.'

She waited for him to look offended, but he didn't. He merely looked thoughtful.

'Well, I suppose that's only to be expected,' he said with surprising cool. 'You don't know me well enough yet to differentiate. But you will, if you give me a chance.'

'I don't think giving you a chance is a good idea. You were right when you said I should forget Gerard. But how could I do that by moving on to his brother? Going out with you would be foolish of me and not fair to you.'

'I don't give a stuff about fairness,' Gerard grated out, startling Leah with his sudden passion. He swivelled further in his seat to take her face in his hands and turn it towards him. 'I don't think you'd be fool-

ish going out with me. Not at all. Stop worrying about
Gerard, Leah, and just go with your heart.'

He kissed her then, and the passion in his voice
was nothing to the passion in his mouth. Leah had
never experienced anything like it. Where Gerard had
seduced, Gareth demanded, prying her lips apart with
a hunger which would not be denied, his tongue driving deep into her mouth. His fingertips tightened on
her cheeks, his thumbs hooking under her chin while
he held her face fiercely captive beneath him.

Not that he needed to hold her captive. She'd been
with him all the way from the moment his mouth had
met hers.

His lips lifted with an abruptness which left her
gasping. They stared at each other, both breathing
heavily. Leah was shocked, for Gareth had just proved
himself a far more passionate man than his brother.

Yet he'd seemed so laid-back last night. A calm,
controlled, self-contained individual. The man staring
at her now with a wildly glittering gaze left Gerard
for dead in the emotional stakes.

'I wanted you from the first moment I saw you,'
he insisted, his turbulent blue eyes laying claim to the
truth of his words.

Leah's head whirled. She'd wanted him from the
first moment she'd seen him as well. But was that
wanting real, or just a replay of what she'd already
experienced with his brother?

Leah hoped for the former, but feared the latter.
Gareth kept telling her to forget Gerard and move on,
but her husband was never going to be forgotten as
easily as that. The last thing she wanted was to hurt

Gareth. But, on the other hand, what if what she was feeling for him *was* real, and her so-called love for Gerard the illusion?

'I won't rush you,' he promised, reaching out to cup her face with gentle hands. 'Just spend some time with me, get to know me.'

She might still have done the noble thing and sent Gareth on his way if he hadn't kissed her again at that moment, this time using a gently persuasive passion to undermine what little defences she had left.

'If Gerard finds out,' she murmured shakily against his very tempting lips, 'he'll go crazy.'

'Why should he find out?'

She drew back then and tried to regather some sense. 'What if that *was* Nigel I saw? What if Gerard's having me watched?'

'Do you honestly believe my brother would be content with having you watched? I know Gerard. If he knew you were here, he'd storm up here in person. Gerard is confrontational. To give him credit, he's not afraid of a fight.'

'If he ever finds me with you, you're the one he'll fight,' Leah warned, shuddering at the thought.

'Gerard doesn't frighten me,' he pronounced with a rather Gerard-like arrogance. 'As I said once before, he deplores violence.'

'He could still ruin your business.'

'He wouldn't dare.'

'You sound very sure of that.'

'Believe me, I am.'

Leah was impressed. Anyone who could stand up

to Gerard impressed her. That took real courage. She hadn't been able to do it.

It crossed her mind, however, that the thought of asking her husband for a divorce did not terrify her as much as it once had. She'd grown stronger during the six months away from him without even realising it. Still, she could not risk going back to Brisbane till she was positive she could face Gerard without the fear of falling victim to his sexual spell once more.

She glanced over at Gareth, not at all sure she wasn't about to fall victim to *his* spell. He was as potently attractive as his brother. Though 'victim' would not be the right word in Gareth's case. No woman would ever be Gareth's victim. She would go willingly into his arms.

'All right,' she said, her voice shaking a little. 'I'll go out with you. But I...I won't promise anything.'

His face registered an astonishingly dark triumph. Dear God, what had she done?

'When?' he demanded to know. 'Tonight, after the cruise? I'll take you to dinner. I'll ask around and book somewhere nice.'

'Nowhere too fancy,' she said swiftly. 'I don't have any fancy clothes.'

'You'd look gorgeous in anything. So when and where will I pick you up?'

'If you drive me home now, I'll show you.'

'It's only one-thirty. Do you really have to go home yet? We could go back to my place. There's a pool there. We could have a swim together.'

Leah was tempted, she had to admit. She felt hot and sticky, sitting in the car. But a swim meant skimpy costumes, and possibly time alone in Gareth's apartment. She wasn't all that confident of his promise not to rush her, not after the way he'd just kissed her.

On top of that, there was something she had to do, something she didn't want to tell Gareth about...

'I really don't have the time,' she said by way of excuse. 'I have some housework to do this afternoon. And some washing.' Which she did. But it wouldn't take her two hours.

Alan always picked her up for work at half past three, after his regular afternoon stop at the pub in town. He drove a small open-air jalopy which he parked at the ready near the far end of Cable Beach, opposite where *The Zephyr* was anchored. He ran her home around seven each night, after the cruise, except for those nights when she stayed aboard. And Mondays, of course. There was no sunset cruise for *The Zephyr* on Mondays.

But today was Friday.

'If you pick me up at eight,' she said, 'I should be ready by then.'

'Eight it is. Now you'd better show me where this place of yours is located.'

CHAPTER SEVEN

THE house Leah shared with the other girls was an ancient wooden white-ant-infested dump. There was no getting around it. How it had survived a hundred years of cyclones she'd no idea.

Admittedly, the dump did have some superficial charm, with its stained glass windows, pitched iron roof and latticed-in verandahs.

The garden was a shambles, however, a tangled mass of trees and shrubs and vines. Half a dozen bougainvillea choked practically everything else, and, while they produced a profusion of brilliant colours at this time of year, their thorns were not to be taken lightly. A couple of times Leah had contemplated doing some pruning, but without proper equipment she would have only ended up scratched and exhausted.

'Pull in over there,' she directed, pointing.

'You live *here*?' Gareth asked, disapproval in his voice as he swung into the rutted driveway, the bumper bar almost hitting the old rusted gates which hung alarmingly outwards.

'It was all I could afford.'

'Mmm. Gerard would not be impressed with his wife living like this.'

'Well, Gerard can go hang himself!'

Gareth laughed, but Leah didn't. Suddenly she wished Gerard would disappear from the face of the earth. She wished she would never have to think of him again. Or see him.

But of course she *would* have to. Even *she* could see that now. One day soon she would have to face him and tell him she wanted a divorce. No easy way out for her. No impersonal solicitor's letter. Otherwise she would never have done with him.

And suddenly that was what she wanted: to have done with him!

How much Gareth had to do with this suddenly intense wish, she didn't know. Maybe she would find some answers in the days to come.

She glanced over at him, her eyes thoughtful. 'How long are you in Broome for, Gareth?'

His blue eyes turned a steely grey as they narrowed. 'For as long as it takes.'

Stubborn, she thought. Just like Gerard.

The realisation rattled her for a moment, till she reminded herself for the umpteenth time that they were identical twins. Gareth himself had admitted they had many similar character traits and tastes. It was inevitable.

Leah also realised she hadn't asked Gareth much about himself as yet. *She'd* been the one doing all the talking. Why hadn't he married, for instance? Why had the brothers stayed estranged? And what of that mysterious mother of theirs, whose very existence Gerard didn't acknowledge?

Leah frowned. What was it Gareth had tried to tell her last night on the boat? Something about Gerard blaming his mother for their father's death.

As much as Leah didn't like bringing up the subject

of Gerard all the time, she might have to one last time. Over dinner tonight, she resolved. Then no more.

'Your company must be doing very well,' she remarked, 'if you can afford to stay here as long as you like.'

'I can't afford not to. I've never met a woman I want as much as I want you, Leah. I know that you and I could have something special together. I won't leave a stone unturned till you let me prove that to you.'

Leah could only shake her head at him. Gerard had rushed her into marriage. She would not let Gareth rush her into *anything*. 'You know, in your own way you're just as stubborn and arrogant as your brother.'

'Is that so bad?'

'Arrogance can make a person one-eyed. Gerard's main failing was he never appreciated how others felt. He never really listened to me when I tried to tell him something. He had his own private agenda in life and everyone else had to fit in with it. I made the mistake of fitting in far too well for far too long. I won't make that same mistake again, with *any* man.'

Gareth's eyes moved over her determined face, and he nodded slowly. 'I can respect that. I won't try to pigeonhole you, Leah. With me, you can be your own person in whatever way you want to be. I promise I'll listen when you tell me something. I won't make the same mistakes Gerard made.'

'But you're his identical twin.'

'I like to think I'm his better half.'

Her eyes saddened. 'I liked to think I was that, once.'

'No more about Gerard,' he suddenly snapped. 'He spoils everything.'

'But there are still some things I must know,' she insisted bravely. 'I was going to ask you over dinner tonight.'

He scowled his displeasure at such an idea.

'You just promised to listen to me,' she reminded him.

He groaned. 'Hung by my own petard!'

Her smile was wry. 'Back to hanging again.'

'Very well,' he agreed grudgingly. 'I'll answer your infernal questions about Gerard. But just this once! Come tomorrow, I want us to start afresh. I want you to look upon me as though we've only just met.'

Impossible, she thought. But didn't say so.

'I want you to give me a real chance to prove to you that I'm nothing like Gerard...except in the things that count.'

'And what are they?'

'I think you already know that, Leah,' he said, with a cool audacity that took her breath away. 'I'm not above using those parts of me which can't fail to impress you. You must have been very attracted to my brother to marry him so quickly.'

'You...you said you wouldn't rush me...'

Even to her ears it sounded a weak protest, and in truth she could not help wondering what it might be like, making love with Gareth. His kiss this afternoon showed he would be a passionate lover. Not as controlled as Gerard. Or compelled to always be on top, both figuratively and literally.

Her train of thought made her whole mouth go dry.

Dear heaven, this was what she'd feared from the start, that she would not be able to resist him!

'I won't rush you,' he promised again. 'But I don't intend to be a wimp, either. I want you, Leah. It's as simple as that.'

She blinked at him. Nothing was as simple as that. Only a man would think so.

'I...I must be going,' she said shakily, and scrambled out of the car before he could kiss her again. She was far too susceptible to his kisses.

'Eight o'clock on the dot,' he called out to her as she hurried up the path.

She waved in answer and hurried in the front door, where she waited for him to leave, her back pressed up against the hallway, her heart hammering in her chest. Only when Gareth had reversed out of the driveway and accelerated away did she race down to her room, snatch up her purse and race out again.

Five minutes later she was standing at one of the payphones on the corner opposite the Commonwealth Bank, dialling a number she knew only too well.

'Sunshine Enterprises,' answered the receptionist after the beeps.

'Mr Woodward, please.'

She was put through to his secretary, as she knew she would be.

'Mr Woodward's office,' came Enid's coolly efficient voice. 'May I help you?'

Leah had always liked Enid, and had felt the liking was returned. She didn't think Enid liked Gerard, however. Leah had glimpsed the odd glance from

Gerard's secretary which suggested she pitied her boss's new bride. Now she understood why.

'Enid. It's Leah.'

Enid's swift intake of breath betrayed her shock. 'Oh, my goodness!' she exclaimed. 'Leah…'

'Yes. Look, I'm sorry to ring you out of the blue like this, but I simply had to.'

'How…how can I help you?'

'Just answer a couple of simple questions for me, please, Enid.'

'I'll do my best.'

'Firstly, is Gerard there, in the office?'

'Well, no…of course he isn't, dear. It's Friday afternoon.'

Leah frowned till she recalled Gerard always wined and dined his top sales executives on a Friday, calling it a business lunch. It usually went on all afternoon.

'So he's not away anywhere?'

'Why would you think that?'

'What about Nigel?' she demanded to know. 'Is he in Brisbane too?'

'He's always where Gerard is, Leah. It would be more than his job is worth not to be on call. Why do you ask?'

'I…I thought I saw Nigel up here.'

'Up where? Where *are* you, Leah? Look, would you like to speak to Gerard? I could ring the restaurant and get him to call you back. I know he'd like to speak to you. Just let me jot down your number and…'

Leah hung up, appalled to find she was shaking from head to toe.

But she gradually calmed down, and once she did she felt so much better. Gerard was still in Brisbane. And he had no idea where she was. That hadn't been Nigel in town, watching her.

She was safe.

Gareth was safe.

At least…for the time being.

CHAPTER EIGHT

LEAH only had one dress in her limited wardrobe. A sundress which could double as a party dress—if you added high heels and jewellery and did your hair nicely.

Made of a cotton knit which didn't crush, the sundress was petticoat-style with a fitted bodice—thankfully lined—narrow shoulder straps and a short flaring skirt that showed off her long tanned legs. The material was a deep orange colour with a multicoloured floral border around the hem which flounced and swirled when she walked.

Leah had bought the dress at the markets again, along with the simple amber-stone pendant which nestled in the deep V of the neckline. The pendant and its matching drop earrings had cost less than some of the cocktails Gerard had used to buy her before dinner at one of his fancy restaurants. The price of the sundress wouldn't have paid for an entrée of oysters.

Despite the designerless quality of her gear, Leah knew she looked rather fetching, so she stayed in her bedroom till Gareth knocked on the door, reluctant to have to put up with her housemates' comments and questions.

Lisa, Cheryl and Dee were so stunned, both by the sight of Leah's handsome date and then by Leah herself, that she sailed past their open-mouthed faces and out through the door before the girls could draw breath.

'As I said,' Gareth murmured when he took her arm. 'You'd look gorgeous in anything.'

He looked pretty gorgeous himself, she thought. Dazzling, actually, dressed in navy trousers and a white open-necked shirt which had tan stitching and tan buttons. A narrow tan leather belt encircled his trim waist, and tan slip-ons covered his feet. The white shirt highlighted his tanned face and arms, as well as his bright blue eyes and glossy black hair.

Gerard had been wearing all white that first day at Hidden Bay, when he'd so impressed her. Leah wondered if his twin knew how well the colour suited him, choosing his clothes deliberately to be at his most attractive for her.

If he had, he'd succeeded. She had to make an effort to drag her eyes away from him as they walked down the path together. He made no such effort, his hungry gaze travelling openly over her from top and toe when he opened the passenger door for her.

'I like your hair done like that,' he complimented her once his eyes returned to her face.

She'd caught it up at the sides, so as to show the earrings, the rest falling down her back in a straight curtain. She hadn't had it cut since leaving Gerard, and her once shoulder-length hair now reached her shoulderblades.

'Thank you,' she said, refusing to look back up at him as she climbed in and clicked the seat-belt in place.

But when he climbed in behind the wheel and

closed the door, her reluctant attention was grabbed, and her head snapped round so she could stare at him.

'Oh!' she exclaimed. 'You...you're not wearing it.

'The cologne,' she added, when he looked blank.

His scent was still very nice, but totally different, a fresh tangy pine perfume wafting from his skin.

His smile was wry. 'Well, a man would have been a fool to keep wearing the other one, don't you think?'

That depended on one's point of view, Leah conceded. It was as well Gareth didn't know why she didn't like him wearing it. Not that the change of cologne was working as well as she might have hoped. She was still overpoweringly aware of the man sitting beside her, especially with the way he kept looking at *her*.

'Well, do you like the new cologne?' Gareth asked, his admiring gaze giving her no peace.

'You smell very nice,' she said tautly. 'Do you think you might drive off? We're being gawked at through the front window.'

'What's the fascination?' Gareth asked as he started the engine and moved off down the road.

'They're not used to my dating. Or dressing up.'

His eyebrows arched. 'So you really haven't gone out with any other men since leaving Gerard?'

'No.'

'You must have been asked.'

'All the time. Especially when I was on the Riviera.'

His sidewards glance showed shock. 'The Riviera? What on earth were you doing there?'

'Scrubbing decks,' she said.

'Scrubbing decks?' he repeated, startled.

'Yep. It paid well, too. The equivalent of fifteen dollars an hour.'

'Yes, but how on earth did you get there?'

'On a boat. A racing yacht.'

'Whose?'

'I have no idea. I was just part of the crew taking it back to France for its wealthy European owners.'

'Wasn't that dangerous?' he asked sharply.

'Not if you knew what you were doing. I've spent most of my life on boats, Gareth. It's as natural to me as breathing. Not only that, it was the best way to me to disappear for a while. Hard to find anyone on the high seas.'

'I can well imagine,' he muttered, and swung the Pajero across the road to the right and shot up a driveway which led to the Mangrove Hotel, an elegant establishment perched on a rise overlooking Roebuck Bay and not far from the place Gareth was staying at.

Leah had heard of its excellent seafood restaurant, but had never been there. In truth, she hadn't been to any restaurants for dinner since she'd arrived in Broome.

'Oh. You're taking me to the Charter's Rest,' she said smilingly.

'Yes. Do you know it?' He angled the car into a spot in the corner of the hotel carpark.

'Only by reputation.'

'I've booked a table for eight-thirty. I'm told there's a good bar next to it where we can have a pre-dinner drink.'

'Lovely.'

He snapped off the engine and turned his face her way, his eyes suddenly intent on hers.

'Yes,' he said huskily, 'you are.'

And, before she could do a thing, he leant over and kissed her on the mouth. Quite lightly, yet for some considerable time, and with devastating effect. She swallowed convulsively when his head finally lifted.

'You…you shouldn't have done that,' she said shakily.

'Why not?'

'Because…' Her eyes were clinging to his, her mind spinning. Because I wanted you to kiss me more than anything from the moment I saw you tonight. Because I know now you're going to kiss me again later this evening. But mostly because by then I won't want you to stop…

He smiled. It was a very Gerard-like smile and disturbed her greatly. 'All's fair in love and war, Leah,' he said.

And then he did something which truly shocked her. He didn't wait till later in the evening, but kissed her again right then and there, looming over her and pinning her to the seat by her shoulders, taking her mouth with a mind-blowing passion which blotted out everything but his lips, and that masterful, marauding tongue.

She flinched when his right hand left her shoulder to cover her knee, then began to move inexorably upwards. Her mind was spinning by the time it reached mid-thigh, sliding over to the smooth soft skin of her inner leg, heading for that part of her which was already burning. She gasped into his mouth, stiffening in a futile defiance of the feelings rampaging through her.

God, but she wanted him to touch her there; wanted his hand to slide inside her underwear and find the hot, wet core of her sex, wanted him to caress it, invade it, seduce it.

Her moan betrayed everything she felt when his hand stopped, then slid back down her leg again. Her desire. Her disappointment. Her dismay.

So when the hand started to slide back up again, her breath caught in her throat, her stomach curling over once more.

But he didn't do what she wanted, just kept caressing her thigh, teasing and tormenting her with his nearness, making her ache with longing as she'd never ached before.

Leah's dismay increased as she accepted how powerless she was to resist him. Utterly powerless. He was an even more skilled seducer than Gerard, she thought dazedly, taking her ever closer to edges in her mind, then leaving her dangling, over and over.

'Sorry,' he said, and abruptly abandoned her. 'I didn't mean things to go quite that far.'

He stared down at her trembling lips, touched them with his fingertips, his head bending slightly again before he jerked himself back into his seat.

'Come on,' he grated out, yanking open his door. 'Let's go get a drink. I think we both need some cooling down.'

Leah's jellied knees almost gave way when her feet touched the ground. Her struggle to stay upright reflected her inner struggle as she battled to put aside the most unnerving sexual arousal she'd ever experienced. It rattled her that Gareth could have done anything he liked to her in that car and she would not have objected. It seemed she was as much a slave to him in that regard as she had been to Gerard.

'Don't be angry with me,' Gareth said as he took her arm and led her tensely silent self across the car-park.

She sighed and halted. 'I'm not angry with you. It's myself I'm angry with.'

'For what reason?'

For being such a weak-willed fool, she thought bitterly. For not knowing what I feel, or for whom. For letting myself get into this impossible situation in the first place.

'For not having stayed and asked Gerard for a divorce,' she said instead. 'I should never have run away. I've only complicated my life terribly.'

'Oh, I don't know, Leah. If you'd never run away, you would never have met me.'

She shook her head. 'I don't think I'm doing you any favours here.'

'Let me be the judge of that.'

'No,' she said. 'I can't keep doing that.'

'What?'

'Letting some man make my decisions for me. I have to start making decisions for myself. And my first is that I'm going to go back to Brisbane next Monday and ask Gerard for a divorce. It's the right thing to do. The only thing. And then I can come back and go out with you with a clear conscience.'

She didn't add that she would know then if Gerard

still had any hold over her heart, would know once and for all if this attraction she felt for Gareth was real, or only a cruel illusion. If Gerard could still get to her, then that would be the end of any relationship with Gareth. She would not use him to assuage a sick obsession for his brother.

And it had to be sick. What woman would continue to love a man who had treated her so shamefully?

Gareth didn't say a word for several moments, but Leah could tell he wasn't happy with her decision.

'Next Monday, you said?'

'Yes, I have most Mondays off. I could fly down first thing in the morning and be back by cruise time on Tuesday evening. I wouldn't like to let Alan down after giving my word to work the full season.'

'Why now?' he said abruptly. 'Is it because of me?'

'Partly.'

'You want to be with me, but you have to be sure you don't still want Gerard too. Is that it?'

'I just want to be free,' she said frustratedly.

'But you *are* free, Leah. Okay, so you're not officially divorced, but you're no longer Gerard's wife. You don't live with him. You left him and you have no intention of ever going back to him. Isn't that right?'

'Yes.'

'Then you're as divorced as any woman with a piece of paper saying she is.'

'I suppose so.'

'Look, if you must go,' he said, 'then I can't stop you. But I don't understand the sudden hurry. We're not lovers yet. I said I wouldn't rush you and I meant it. Trust me, Leah.'

'Words will never be enough for me any more, Gareth. Actions speak much more loudly. What you did to me in that car was the action of a man intent on having his way. I know seduction when I feel it. I was well acquainted with it in my marriage.'

He winced at her last words. 'It wasn't my intention to seduce you,' he muttered. 'Believe me, if it was, I would not have stopped. I simply got carried away with the moment. That's the truth of the matter. You're a very beautiful and desirable woman, Leah, and I'm only human. But I promise to do better in future. Come on, let's go inside, with other people and out of temptation.'

CHAPTER NINE

THE bar was separate from the restaurant, quite a large room, with a tropically colonial feel to its decor.

Called The Palms, it had a large bar with brass railings across one end, where a few people were perched up on fabric-covered stools, with serviceable grey tiles underfoot. Dark carpet covered the rest of the floor on which stood cream-coloured tables surrounded by pale cane-backed chairs. Three upturned beer barrels down the middle of the room also served as tables, one flanked by two elderly gentlemen playing a game of chess.

The far wall was mainly glass and overlooked a terrace beyond which lay a lawn courtyard, fringed by palms and lit with ball-lights on tall green poles. The bay beyond was not visible, its mangrove-lined waters as dark as the night sky.

'Where would you like to sit?' Gareth asked.

Hardly any of the tables were occupied, most of the evening's patrons probably having moved on to dinner by then.

Leah chose one of the empty tables against the glass wall.

'What would you like to drink?'

His offer startled her. Gerard had rarely asked her what she wanted to drink, though she conceded that was partly her own fault. In the beginning she hadn't known what to order, always deferring to him.

'A gin and tonic would be nice.' Gin and tonic had become her favourite drink during her travels abroad. Her time had mostly been spent in hot humid harbours. A tall gin and tonic with plenty of ice had been a refreshing drink at the end of a hard day mending sails or swabbing decks.

When Gareth turned to walk over to the bar she watched him go, her gaze running over him from behind. He had a very nice behind. No doubt he had a very nice everything, just like his brother.

Leah pursed her lips in aggravation at always comparing the two brothers. It really was an impossible situation, one which asking Gerard for a divorce would probably not cure. Gerard would always lie between any relationship she formed with Gareth. It would be like having a ghost around all the time, a third in their bed. At least for her…

Leah put her elbows on the table, her head coming to rest in her hands, her eyes closing. Whatever was she going to do?

'You're thinking of Gerard again.'

Leah's head snapped up at Gareth's voice, her elbows shooting back off the table.

'You were quick,' she said, ignoring his comment about Gerard.

His face showed extreme irritation as he placed her gin and tonic in front of her and sat down with a beer.

'Let's get one thing straight,' he said firmly. 'Do you or do you not still love him?

'I want the truth now,' he demanded when she hesitated.

'I don't honestly know, Gareth,' she admitted, and started sipping her drink through the straw. 'Maybe. Maybe not.'

'You said you despised him.'

'I do.'

'In that case you don't love him.'

She could only shake her head. 'He was my first love, Gareth. My first lover...'

'But surely when you heard what you heard any love for him would have died.'

'Yes, you would have thought so. It's just that...'

'Just what?'

'I don't think you will want to hear this next part.'

'I want to hear everything about you and Gerard, Leah. What happened between you two is vital to what happens between us.'

'Yes, I suppose so,' she said, returning to her drink for a deeper swallow.

'Then just spit it out. I can take it.'

Leah put aside the straw and looked into Gareth's eyes. 'I was going to confront Gerard the night I overheard him saying what he said. I meant to. But when he came upstairs that night he...he didn't give me much of a chance. He started making love to me and I...I...'

'Yes?' Gareth asked tensely, the beer clutched, untouched, between his hands.

'I simply forgot about what he'd said. I forgot everything but the moment...the pleasure. Then afterwards I felt so humiliated, so...ashamed. I realised then I wasn't strong enough to fight Gerard on open terms. Whether it was love or not, whatever I felt for him was too powerful. *He* was too powerful.'

'I see.'

'No, you *don't* see!' she snapped. 'He proved that power again the following night even more horribly. I'd already made my plans to leave him, but it was going to be a couple more days before I could physically leave the house. I invented a headache to get out of making love, but he got round me again, seducing me quite effortlessly. And I enjoyed it, Gareth. Mindlessly. Madly. I cried myself to sleep afterwards.'

'Hell, Leah.'

'Don't worry, it disgusted me just as much as it's disgusting you. So, on the last night I decided I would not let him seduce me again. I could not have borne it. So I did something I'd never done before. I...well, suffice it to say I took the initiative. And he was so darned pleased, not knowing how much it killed me to do such a thing.'

Tears welled up in her eyes as she thought of that night again, and the subsequent tenderness Gerard had put into his lovemaking. Any woman would have believed he'd loved her then.

But he *hadn't*! reminded the cold voice of reason.

Good God, how much suffering did it take for her to ram that simple fact into her thick skull, to put aside her feelings for the man and get on with her life?

She blinked the tears away with a fierce burst of

pride, the reliving having reinforced her resolve to have done with Gerard.

'I'm sorry, Gareth,' she said. 'I should not have told you that. It wasn't fair to you.'

'You're wrong, Leah. You should have. I now understand why you ran away from Gerard. I hated thinking you were afraid he might do you physical harm. Other than that, what you've told me is nothing more than I already knew. Gerard is a very experienced and skilful lover.'

'Yes, but…but…'

'But nothing,' he said, overriding any protest. 'I'll be an even better lover. Because I truly care about you. I won't be just trying to prove I'm better than Casanova. Now drink up, darling. Our dinner reservation awaits.'

Leah went in to dinner in a rather dazed state. She'd thought Gerard was a stubborn man. And supremely self-confident. But his brother left him in the shade!

'You're incorrigible,' she muttered to Gareth as they followed the waitress to a table in the non-smoking section.

'Yes,' he returned simply. 'My mother says the same.'

The non-smoking section was a glassed-in nook which resembled a conservatory and overlooked the courtyard from a different angle. The carpet was bluish, the walls cream, the tables covered in rusty coloured tablecloths with a cream overlay, a brass-bottomed candle-holder in the middle of each.

There were several marine souvenirs dotted around the room, Leah especially liking a brass diving bell hat which rested on a nearby counter—a relic from the days when brave men had dived deep into the sea to bring the highly prized pearl shells to the surface.

Brass ceiling fans and colonial wall-lights completed the stylish old-world elegance. Anywhere else in the world Leah might have felt under-dressed in such a setting, but here, in Broome, everything was far more casual.

The waitress, who was dressed in flowing black trousers and a simple white blouse, pulled out the cane-backed chairs for them at their table for two, then waited while they sat down before handing Leah the food menu and Gerard the wine list.

'A Chablis do?' Gerard asked after a swift perusal. 'Or would you prefer a Chardonnay?'

'Not Chardonnay,' she said.

Gareth frowned at her sharp tone, then shrugged and selected a local West Australian Chablis, the waitress hurrying off to do his bidding as waitresses had been hurrying off to do handsome men's bidding for centuries.

'You don't like Chardonnay?' he asked.

'No, I don't,' she said, then quickly buried her head in the dinner menu.

Gerard had never ordered her any other white wine but Chardonnay, which had a tendency to go straight to her head. He rather liked her tipsy, he'd once told her as he'd pulled his black Porsche over into a darkened side road on the way home from a dinner party. She was always deliciously co-operative that way, he'd added as he'd switched off the darkly throbbing engine and turned to her.

'Deliciously co-operative', she thought angrily, her upper lip curling with self-contempt. Downright gullible, more like it. A push-over!

'None of the food to your liking?' Gareth asked, misinterpreting her expression.

'Oh, no, no, it's all lovely food. I just don't know what to order.' God, but she was flushing, heat filling her face as what had happened in the car that night flashed into her mind.

Leah was eternally grateful the room wasn't too brightly lit!

'What about good old fish and chips?' Gareth suggested, smiling.

Her laugh sounded strained. 'I don't think that's on the menu. Here. You order this time. I can't seem to make up my mind all of a sudden.'

Or any other time, came a brutal inner voice.

If Gerard were sitting opposite you right now, you probably *would* go to mush. He wouldn't have to touch you. He'd only have to look at you and tell you with his eyes what he'd like to be doing to you—or what he'd like *you* to be doing to *him*—and you'd be incapable of either speech or simple thought.

She glanced over the candle to where Gareth was studying the menu, his classically formed features etched into planes and angles by the flickering candle-light.

'Do you look like your father or your mother?' she asked abruptly.

Her head jerked up, his eyes startled. 'My father. Why?'

'Tell me about them.'

'What about them?'

'I want to know everything.'

'That's a tall order—even worse than deciding what we'll eat tonight.' He folded the menu and immediately the waitress was at his side, wanting to know if he wished to order.

In contradiction of his supposed indecision, he crisply ordered spicy Thai pumpkin soup for starters, to be followed by Barramundi wings in lemon butter and caper sauce. He agreed to a suggestion of the waitress for herb bread, but refused dessert at that time—a decision to be made later.

When the waitress had departed he looked thoughtful for a moment, then began fiddling with his fork, drawing patterns on the tablecloth. Leah waited for him to speak first, shifting a little nervously in her seat.

'My father was a carpenter,' he began. 'You know the song about the carpenter in love with the lady? He asks her if she would marry him and have his baby. That was similar to my parents' marriage. He was a carpenter and she was a lady. Only she married him *because* she was having his baby.'

'Babies,' Leah corrected.

'What? Oh, yes, well, she didn't know that at the time. This was pre-ultrasound. Anyway, it was a disastrous mismatch from the start. Or so I finally realised.'

'What do you mean, finally? Weren't you boys aware your parents didn't get along?'

'Not really. My mother was a lady, remember? She'd been brought up to always be perfectly polite, to always look perfect and to always defer to the menfolk in her life. The façade was more important than the reality. I thought she and Dad were happy enough. I had no idea they were both miserable.

'Mum felt trapped, and Dad was tormented by thoughts she might leave him one day. He knew, you see, that she didn't love him, that he'd just been a mad rebellious fling, that she'd only married him because of her pregnancy. He, however, was crazy about her. He thought if he gained wealth, he might buy her love.

'Unfortunately, he didn't have a business brain. He tried everything but only ever succeeded in losing more money. Mum had to go out to work to make ends meet. Towards the end he began to drink heavily. Then one day, about ten years ago, when he was in a drunken rage, he beat her very badly. And she left him.'

'Ten years ago,' Leah repeated slowly, frowning. 'That was when you and Gerard parted company, wasn't it?'

'Just about then.'

'What happened exactly?'

'The day my mother left, Gerard and I came home to find my father drunk and Mum gone. Dad told us a pack of lies about how he'd found out she'd been having an affair with her wealthy boss for years, that the boss's wife had finally died and he wanted to marry Mum, that she'd left without a backward glance, not caring about any of us any more.

'He ranted and raved about how she'd always despised being married to a man who worked with his hands, that all she'd wanted out of life was money and material things. He claimed he'd worked his fingers to the bone to provide for her but nothing was ever good enough.

'Naturally, this all came as a bit of shock. As I said, their marriage had seemed reasonably happy on the surface.'

'But you believed him?'

'Gerard did. He'd had a recent experience with a girl dumping him for a guy with a sports car, so I guess he was rather primed to believe badly of women. He'd never been all that close to Mum, either. Dad had been the better parent, affectionate and loving. Mum was far more remote, emotionally. On top of that, things did look damaging against her.

'Without us seeing her bruises, we had no idea what Dad had done. He'd never even hit her before. She hadn't left any letter for us. Neither did she ring up at that time and explain. We didn't know it then, but she was terrified Dad might murder her. He'd already threatened to kill her, and had actually gone to her boss's home with a loaded rifle.'

'So she *was* at her boss's house?'

'Yes. He was very fond of her. He doesn't deny that, even today. But he swears they were never lovers. Mum had gone to him for protection when she had nowhere else to turn and he'd taken her in. It wasn't till later that they fell in love. Still, her being in his home was another nail in her coffin in Gerard's opinion. He went to the house himself. It was a mansion down on the Gold Coast. Unfortunately, by then Mum and her boss had left for the States together.'

'That must have looked pretty bad.'

'It did. When Dad found out he went crazy. He wouldn't believe Gerard. He accused him of lying. He raced out to the garage, jumped in his utility and screamed off at a suicidal speed. He crashed it on the way and was declared dead on arrival at the hospital.'

'Oh, Gareth…how awful.'

'It was. It really was…'

'So, did your mother contact you eventually?'

'Yes.'

'And?'

'Gerard wouldn't speak to her, wouldn't listen. He blamed her for Dad's death. In the end she gave up trying to explain to him. When she actually married her boss, Gerard saw that as final and irretrievable proof that our father had been the wronged party. He told me that he never wanted to see her or speak to her again. She was dead as far as he was concerned.'

Leah could only shake her head. She could imagine Gerard saying that. Once crossed, he would never forgive or forget. No doubt he hated *her* now.

'He changed after that,' Gareth went on. 'He became ruthlessly ambitious. He dropped out of architecture and—'

'Gerard was an architect too?' Leah broke in, startled.

'He was. But after Dad's death being a fledgling architect just wouldn't do. Not enough money in it. So he went into sales. Selling houses proved far more lucrative than designing them. He worked seven days a week. Had no time for the things we'd once planned

to do together. He had no time for me at all. I was a
constant reminder of what had happened to Dad.'

'So he cut you out of his life! And his mother as
well!'

'He believed she'd lied.'

'Isn't that just like Gerard?' Leah went on with a
wealth of feeling. '*You* had the decency to hear your
mother's point of view and keep an open mind. But
Gerard only has one point of view. *His.*'

Gareth frowned. 'I was hoping you might understand your husband a little better once you knew his
background. I was hoping you might have it in your
heart to forgive him.'

'Never!' she exclaimed heatedly. 'God, no. How
can you possibly ask that of me, Gareth? What he did
to me was unforgivable. I don't care what his background was. I'm sick and tired of people finding excuses for their actions because of something that happened in the past. Once you become an adult you
make your own choices and decisions. *Your* background was the same as Gerard's and you didn't turn
out to be a cold-blooded conscienceless devil. No, I
can't excuse him. He knew what he was doing and
he did it anyway.'

'Mmm. That's an impressive speech, Leah, and I
understand where you're coming from, but things can
be straightforward in theory yet not so easy to put
into practice. You're guilty yourself of letting the past
colour your present actions. That's why you're hiding
away in this remote corner of the world.'

Leah flinched, stung by Gareth's cool reasoning.
But then she rallied. 'I think I can be forgiven for

going to ground for six months. That's a lot shorter time span than ten years. Besides,' she added, her chin lifting, 'I *don't* intend to keep hiding away. As I already told you, I am going to go back to Brisbane and ask Gerard for a divorce. Next Monday. After that, I'll happily go home.'

'I thought you said you didn't want to let Alan down.'

'Alan won't have any trouble finding a replacement if I give him a few days' notice. My job hardly requires a degree in either sailing or catering.'

'I couldn't do it,' he said drily.

'Yes, well, working on a boat is a bit silly if you get seasick.'

'I don't get seasick.'

Leah was taken aback. 'But last night…when you came down below…after you went to the bathroom…you…you looked quite ill.'

'I *felt* ill. I'd just witnessed that cosy little scene between you and Alan on deck, which I was already struggling to handle, then I walked past your boss's cabin and saw his double bed, unmade and rumpled as only two lovers could have made it. I can only tell you I was almost sick on the spot.'

'He'd had a lady-friend stay the previous night,' Leah explained, shaken by the extent of his passion for her. He'd felt so strongly about her even then, within an hour or two of their meeting?

Amazing!

'Why not put off going back to Brisbane till I can go with you?' he suggested. 'We could fly back on the same plane.'

'When's your return flight?'

'I was originally planning on staying here two weeks.'

'What do you mean…originally?'

'After I met you, I changed my plans.'

'Whatever am I going to do with you, Gareth?' she said, shaking her head at him.

'I could give you heaps of suggestions,' he drawled, and looked deep into her eyes.

The arrival of the pumpkin soup and herb bread rescued Leah. But not for long.

'Do me a favour and forget about Gerard for a while,' Gareth said abruptly once the waitress had departed. 'You have the rest of your life to ask for a divorce. All I want is two or three weeks without any hangovers from the past. Is that too much to ask?'

'I guess not…'

'I want you to pretend we've only just met.'

'We *have* only just met!'

'Don't split hairs, Leah.' And he set his eyes upon her once more, those intensely penetrating blue eyes. 'An eternity can be fitted into a few hours.'

Something twisted deep inside Leah, something far too darkly sexual for her peace of mind. This was worse than when Gerard had looked at her across a dinner table. Far worse. Back then she'd waited like a good little girl for her husband to do the seducing. Now she was besieged with thoughts of what *she* might do to his brother when they left this restaurant.

'I'm going out to the Willie Creek Pearl Farm tomorrow morning,' Gareth said as he picked up a chunk of herb bread and broke it apart in his fingers. 'Will you come with me?'

The Willie Creek Pearl Farm was the only cultured pearling establishment around Broome which catered for tourists, doing tours morning and afternoon. Leah had already been once and found it fascinating, especially seeing the way they seeded the live oyster shells to make pearls. They had a fine showroom of locally handcrafted jewellery as well. Not that she'd bought anything. But Gareth might like to buy something for his mother.

An innocent enough outing, she decided. They would not be alone. Leah didn't want to be really alone with Gareth. Not yet. As much as she wanted him, she knew sex with Gareth would confuse her even more.

'All right,' she agreed at last.

'You had to think about it long enough,' he grumbled. 'What was the problem?'

'No problem.'

'Better eat your soup, then, before it gets cold.'

Leah was only too happy to eat her soup. She was only too happy to have a whole meal to devour. Only too happy to be in a very public place where nothing could come of the thoughts running through her mind, and the unchecked desires running through her veins.

But she knew, even when the night came to a thankfully uneventful end, with Gareth amazingly not trying anything when he took her home—other than a goodnight peck—that it was probably only a matter of time before she went to bed with him.

No, not a bed, her mind amended later that night

as she lay, wide awake, staring blankly up at the ceiling fan. She wanted to have him where she could see every inch of that beautiful body of his. Not between sheets. Out on the deck of *The Zephyr* perhaps, in the moonlight, under the stars…

CHAPTER TEN

'SO WHAT have you been up to all day?' Alan asked, glancing over at Leah.

They were bumping down the dirt road which led to Gantheaume Point and the spot where Alan parked his jalopy every night. It was three-thirty in the afternoon, and a mild sea breeze was blowing.

'Oh, this and that,' she returned noncommittally, though smiling with pleasure at the memory of the day spent with Gareth.

They'd had such fun that morning out at the pearling farm. They'd driven out together in Gareth's Pajero, but joined up with a party of tourists once they got there.

Everyone had been a bit subdued to begin with, the mostly elderly group traipsing around after the man conducting the tour like chastened schoolchildren. But when Gareth had started asking questions everyone else had suddenly come to life, chatting and laughing together, taking photographs and asking even more questions.

They'd had a delightful mid-morning break of damper bread and drinks on the verandah of the owner's lovely house before strolling through the showroom where she'd turned down Gareth's offer to buy her something. He'd seemed pleased when she'd told him she wanted nothing from him but his company.

When the tour had ended, they'd driven to Cable Beach to have lunch, sitting on the grass under the palms and talking about silly things. Nothing heavy at all. Gerard had not been mentioned once, and had rarely entered Leah's thoughts.

Afterwards, they'd strolled along the beach, hand in hand. Leah had found the experience warm and sweet, and not too sexually tense, although things had become momentarily strained when they'd come across another couple walking towards them, stark naked.

Cable Beach was a well-known spot for nudists, but this couple hadn't exactly been hiding in the sandhills or lying discreetly face-down in the sand. Naturally they'd had good bodies, otherwise they probably wouldn't have been making an exhibition of themselves.

'Just what I need,' Gareth had muttered under his breath.

'Fancy her, do you?' Leah had teased, trying to break the instant tension between them.

'Nah,' he'd mocked back. 'But the bloke isn't half bad.'

They'd both dissolved into giggles, which had brought a haughty look from the woman and a glare from the man.

Leah grinned at the memory.

'Well, whatever "this and that" was,' Alan said drily, 'he's put a happy look on your face. Which is good to see.'

'What makes you think it's a he?'

'Honey, you're talkin' to good ole Alan here. If anyone knows what makes a female tick, it's me. Which reminds me...could you mind the boat for me tonight?'

Leah's face fell. Gareth had asked her out to dinner again tonight.

'Okay, okay, I get the picture,' Alan said in droll tones. 'The boyfriend has plans for you tonight. So perhaps we could find a compromise?'

They'd reached Alan's parking spot, the dust settling around them now that the wheels had stopped turning on the dirt road.

'What kind of compromise?'

'Is he a tourist?'

'What?'

'The boyfriend. Is he a tourist?'

'Yes...' No way was she going to tell Alan who, exactly.

'Do you know where he's staying?'

'Well...yes. The Roebuck Bay apartments. Why?'

'I'll ring him from my mobile phone right now and we'll sort something out.' He started punching in the number. 'What's his name?'

Leah bit her bottom lip. Alan frowned before his expression suddenly cleared. 'Good God, it isn't? Not your ex's *brother*!'

Her guilty face told it all. Alan put his finger on the 'off' button.

'Leah, Leah...if what you said about the ex is true, then you're playing with fire. This is the sort of scenario Greek tragedies are made of.'

'I'm not sleeping with him!'

'Not yet, you mean. But I know that look on a woman.'

'What look?'

'That he's-crazy-about-me and I'd-like-to-eat-him-up look.'

Leah winced. 'Does it show that badly?'

'Yes.'

'I know it's an awkward situation,' she admitted with a ragged sigh. 'He says he wants me more than any woman he's ever met.'

'Mmm. That's a good line. I've used it myself.'

'It's not a line, Alan. Gareth's no conman like his brother. If he was, he'd have sworn love at first sight and swept me into bed. I told him I wasn't sure which brother I was really attracted to and he said he's not at all worried. He's supremely confident I will eventually choose him. In truth, Alan, he's everything I could possibly want in a man. If I'd met him first, I know I would have fallen for him. But everything is clouded by my having fallen in love with and married Gerard first. Gerard is not a man easily forgotten.'

'Monsters rarely are,' Alan pointed out drily. 'They can be such fascinating creatures.'

Leah shuddered. Yes, Alan was right. Gerard had fascinated her from the start. But that fascination had blinded her to the real man underneath. The monster.

'How can I tell if what I feel for Gareth is the real thing, Alan?' she asked, her eyes pleading with him for an answer. 'Or just an illusion?'

'Am I right in presuming you lust after both brothers like mad?'

'Oh, God, it sounds awful when you say it like that. But I do. I *like* Gareth a lot more, though. He's much nicer. Sweeter. Softer.'

'Not too soft, I hope,' Alan muttered drily, and Leah blushed. 'Look, Leah, sometimes lust is best confronted. Your feelings often clarify after you've been to bed with someone. I guarantee by morning you'll know which brother you prefer, in bed and out. A man reveals a lot about himself when he makes love.'

'You think so?'

'I know so. Now, shall I ring Gareth and offer him a free night on *The Zephyr* with his own private and very pretty serving girl? I'll even put clean sheets on the bed in the master cabin,' he added with a wickedly saucy grin.

Leah didn't know what to say. To have Alan make such an offer with her approval was tantamount to agreeing to let Gareth make love to her.

The thought blew her away. She wanted him, but she was terrified of the consequences.

'A lady can always say no, Leah,' Alan said on seeing her instant panic. 'It's a big boat. Your inviting him to share its beauty for a night is not necessarily an invitation to share more. Make that clear to him when he comes aboard. If he's the nice man you say he is, he'll respect that, won't he?'

Yes, she thought. He would. Gareth was not like Gerard. He was not a monster.

'All right,' she said, and let out a long-held breath. 'Ring up and ask him.'

Gareth was coming, Alan told her a couple of
minutes later. With bells on.

He wasn't wearing bells when he stepped from the
Zodiac onto the deck of *The Zephyr* at seven-thirty
that evening. He wasn't wearing very much at all,
Leah thought, a lump forming in her throat as she
looked him over. Bright board shorts. A blue singlet
top with 'Broome' emblazoned across his very nice
chest in iridescent yellow letters. And leather thongs
which he immediately shook off his bare feet.

She wasn't wearing much more, she supposed. She
did keep *some* spare clothes on board, but not many.
After Alan had left earlier, to take the cruise party
back to shore, she'd dashed down below, stripped off
the shorts and top she'd had on all day and showered
at length.

The pink shorts she was now wearing were short
shorts, just covering her buttocks. The T-shirt was
modest enough, however, white and baggy, with large
pink hibiscus flowers providing some refuge for her
braless breasts, both of which were suddenly feeling
very vulnerable. She almost wished she'd left her hair
down instead of scooping its damp mass up into a
high ponytail. She could hide a fair bit when her hair
was down these days.

'Thanks, Alan,' Gareth called out, waving towards
where the Zodiac was already speeding across the water back to shore. He turned to face her, lifting up his
other hand which was laden with two heavy-looking
plastic bags.

'Chinese,' he said, smiling. 'And champagne. The best.'

'You shouldn't have.' She tried to smile back, but it felt like a grimace. Of all the times for Gareth to sound just like his brother. Gerard had always bought the best. Of everything.

'Why not? You deserve the best.'

Her heart flipped over. Now *that* was nothing like Gerard. He'd only ever bought the best as a reflection of his wealth and success, never for anyone else.

Now her smile was real. 'I meant the Chinese, silly. I was going to cook something. Alan has a very well-equipped larder on board.'

'Not tonight. Tonight I don't want you to do anything except lie back and relax.'

Leah only heard the words 'lie back'. She knew she had to say something before it was too late. 'Gareth,' she began tautly, while the rest of her body thrummed, 'I don't want you to think that inviting you here for the night was an invitation to…to…'

'Hey,' he interrupted softly. 'I said relax, remember? You call the shots. I won't be doing anything you don't want me to do.'

'But that's the trouble,' she muttered agitatedly. 'I *do* want you to.'

His eyes darkened appreciably. 'I wish you hadn't said that…'

'I wish I hadn't too,' she groaned. 'Oh God, this is dreadful.'

'No, it isn't dreadful.' Gareth placed the plastic bags down on the deck then came forward to curve gentle but firm hands over her shoulders. 'It's inevitable,' he murmured, and gathered her close, his mouth dipping to cover hers, his dark head blotting out the moon, his kiss blotting out everything for Leah but his lips and his tongue and his hard male body pressed against hers.

Her reaction was the same as it had been the other day. She was besieged with instant need. And a hunger which obliterated everything but the moment.

'No, don't,' Leah moaned when his mouth lifted temporarily for breath.

'Don't what?' he whispered back while his mouth rained wet kisses over her face and neck.

'Don't stop.'

He just laughed, then startled her by gripping the bottom of her T-shirt in both his hands and stripping it up over her head and ponytail, then tossing it away onto the deck.

The feel of the night air on her bare breasts was arousing in the extreme. His hot eyes on them sent her pulse-rate haywire. His hands on them brought a dark haze down over her conscious mind. His *mouth* on them banished every mixed-up thought she'd had these past few days and which were still lurking in her mind, ready to spoil things.

Gerard. Gareth. It didn't seem to matter who it was, making her feel like this. She moaned in recognition of the overwhelming nature of her erotic intoxication. All she wanted at that moment was for that tormenting tongue to keep lapping at her rock-hard nipples, those tantalising teeth to make her cry out with pained pleasure, those all-engulfing lips to suckle her breast ever deeper into his mouth.

She groaned when that hot, wet mouth abandoned her breasts and began sliding down towards her stomach, when *he* began to sink down, down onto his knees, taking her shorts and G-string with him, stripping her totally of her clothes and her conscience.

The shorts and G-string went the same way as her top, and she found herself leaning against the bulwark, naked and panting. A still kneeling Gareth pushed her legs apart, caressed and kissed the tops of her thighs, then between her thighs, knowing exactly where to probe, to lick, to suck, instinctively honing in on that spot that drove her wild.

Her hands clutched at the ropes on either side of her as she moaned her frenzy, her back arching, her thighs quivering. She squeezed her eyes shut, trying not to come too soon, and just as she was certain she must hurtle over into that abyss of darkly shuddering ecstasy he stood up, taking her with him, lifting her up to sit on the railing.

Her eyes remained wide on him when he let her go to divest himself of his shorts. The scar from his accident shone white under the moonlight. But it wasn't his scar which held her dry-mouthed gaze.

Leah swallowed when he moved back between her legs, gasped when his flesh met hers, groaned when he surged deep inside.

She came immediately, her own flesh clasping and unclasping his as she cried out, then just cried, sobbing with her release against his shoulder. He cradled her to him for a long while, then carried her down below, their bodies still joined.

'In here?' he indicated brusquely, nodding towards

the main cabin where Alan had made up the bed with clean sheets. In fact, that was all there was on the bed. Sheets, and half a dozen pillows. Some small recessed lights in the wall above the bed lent just enough light to see by.

She nodded in dazed agreement and Gareth angled her inside the narrow doorway before lying them both down on the bed, Leah underneath him, her legs still wrapped around his hips.

Leah was fiercely aware that he hadn't come, his body still deliciously big and hard within her. His control amazed her, as did her own rapidly returning desire. She'd never felt like this so soon after having a climax before. She usually took ages to be turned on again, but her body seemed to be craving Gareth even more for having been satisfied once.

She wanted him to move, wanted to feel his flesh filling hers before partly withdrawing then plunging back in, deeper and deeper. Her heartbeat quickened at the thought, her lips parting, her mouth and throat drying as a shallow panting escaped her lungs. Her legs tightened around him while her tongue swept out and over her parched lips.

Gareth watched the action from where he was leaning over her, his elbows on either side of her tensing body, his hands cupping her face.

'Let me,' he said, his mouth descending to wet her lips with slow, seductive licks of his tongue.

Her mouth gasped open wider, inviting him, begging him.

At last he obliged, his tongue sinking slowly into the waiting cavern, sliding down the centre of *her* tongue before curling up and raking the tip over the sensitive skin of her palate. He repeated the action over and over till she was beside herself with wanting, her hips lifting off the bed in an effort to take him deeper into her body. She moaned her frustration, her hands lifting to rake her fingers through his hair, her eyes wide and pleading upon him.

At last his mouth lifted and he began to move within her, doing exactly what she wanted, but slowly. So very, very slowly. The feelings he evoked were exquisite as he undulated within her, withdrawing almost to the point of no return before sinking back down into her depths. She felt as if she was floating on a sea of pleasure, cresting with the waves before dropping down into the troughs.

Gradually, however, the sea turned stormy. She was cresting higher, crashing down lower. Her nails dug into his back; her back arched up from the bed.

'Oh!' she cried out as a fierce spasm sliced through her flesh.

'Leah,' Gareth groaned, and exploded inside her, his whole body trembling violently.

She was beyond replying, beyond anything but holding him to her, savouring her own sensations, *and* his, rocking her hips against his as he came, and came, and came.

At last he was still, collapsed across her, his lips in her hair. Leah lay beneath him, wallowing in his weight, and his flooding warmth.

The thought finally infiltrated that this was how silly women had unwanted babies, by allowing themselves to be carried away in the heat of the moment.

But, oh, the glory of that heat! And that moment! She could not have stopped him for the world. Thank heavens a baby was unlikely tonight!

Her hands splayed across his back as she held him close to her. She murmured his name as she kissed his shoulder. 'Gareth…'

Yes, it was Gareth she wanted, she decided with an astonishing mixture of satisfaction and as yet unsated desires.

Not Gerard.

Gareth.

CHAPTER ELEVEN

'NO, DON'T,' Gareth said, flinching when Leah touched a soft fingertip to his scar.

'But I don't find it ugly or anything,' she murmured. 'Nothing about you could possibly be ugly.'

They were lying out on the deck in the stern of the boat behind the wheel. Leah had brought up a few duvets from the bunks below and made a type of mattress for them to lie on under the stars. Gareth was stretched out on his back and she was on her side, propped up on one elbow.

'I want to look at all of you,' she murmured thickly. 'Touch all of you. Kiss all of you...'

She had wanted to do all of those things in the shower they'd just tried to share, but there was hardly room for one in the tiny cubicle, let alone two. Gareth's sheer size had made things impossible and in the end they'd showered separately, any fantasy Leah had had about the shower providing some exciting intimacies temporarily put aside.

Not so now. Gareth was lying there magnificently naked and totally at her disposal.

He groaned when she went perilously close to his rapidly reviving penis, and once again Leah's thoughts flew to Gerard.

He'd never groaned when they made love. Had never made a sound. The sounds had all come from her. The moans and groans, the pleas and cries, the gasps and sighs. Stung by this thought, Leah decided she liked hearing Gareth groan, and sought to make him groan some more.

She ran a fingernail up and down the length of him, ever so lightly. His flesh fairly jumped, and the sound he made sent an erotic shiver rippling down her spine. She touched him again, but not with her fingernail this time. Three soft fingertips skimmed over the straining flesh, followed by her whole hand, encircling him, teasing him, tormenting him.

Soon it wasn't the sounds coming from Gareth's throat which enthralled Leah but her own arousal. A hot twisting ache was gripping her between her legs and her nipples were standing on end, impatient in their need to be caressed. Leaning down, she rubbed the sensitive peaks all over him, then cupped her hanging breasts around him, rocking backwards and forwards, squeezing the swollen curves into a type of tunnel into which he was thrusting. She heard his raw panting breaths, felt his body stiffen, heard his cry of warning. But she didn't care. She was as much out of control as he was.

She climaxed when he did, without his having laid a finger on her.

Leah lay there afterwards, stunned. Gareth was so-licitous in his care of her, cleaning her gently with a warm flannel he brought from below, then drying her with a towel. When she began to shiver he covered her with one of the duvets then slipped in to cuddle her close.

'You all right?' he asked gently.

'I…I don't know…' She felt she was unravelling. Her head. Her body. Amazingly she still wanted him, wanted to do even more things to him, things she'd had to be persuaded to do for Gerard, and some things she'd *never* done. My God, she'd become a wild woman. A wanton. A…a nymphomaniac!

'Don't be embarrassed, Leah,' he murmured. 'What you did was beautiful and incredibly passionate. I loved it. *You* loved it. That's because we love each other.'

She turned to look at him in surprise, saw the love for her shining in his eyes, felt her own heart lurch in response.

'I loved you from the first moment I saw you,' he said thickly.

Tears sprang to her eyes at the memory of Gerard saying that to her, more than once. Only with Gerard it hadn't been true.

'You really mean that?' she choked out.

'I've never meant anything more in my life.'

Sincerity blazed within the blue of his eyes. Sincerity and the most heart-rending appeal.

'Say you love me too, Leah. I couldn't bear it if you didn't.'

'Oh, Gareth!' she cried, and threw her arms around his neck. 'I do,' she sobbed. 'I can see that now. I love you so much it's like an ache deep inside me that never seems to be satisfied. I love you so much it…it frightens me.'

'Don't let it, darling,' he soothed, easing her back down onto the duvet and smoothing a few strands of hair back from her flushed face. 'I feel the same way about you. Believe me when I say all I want is to love you, and look after you.'

'Yes, yes, I *do* believe you. You'd never do what your brother did. You'd never lie to me, or try to con me. Why, there's not a bad bone in your whole body!' And she snuggled into him, kissing his chest, his throat, his chin.

'Leah...'

'Yes, my darling?' She glanced up, smiling, and saw his serious face. Her alarm was instant, making her stomach churn. 'What is it? What's the matter?'

He didn't say a word, his eyes darkly troubled. Leah just knew he was thinking about Gerard. He'd said he wasn't worried about his brother but she knew he was. She resolved then and there to do something about Gerard herself. He was *her* problem, after all.

'Don't think of Gerard tonight, Gareth,' she advised, her heart full of love for this man. 'He'll only spoil things, like you said. We'll worry about him later.'

'Later,' he repeated, still looking anxious. 'The trouble is, Leah, later always comes. And sometimes later is not better.'

'Do you want us to both go down and tell Gerard straight away?'

He actually shuddered. Leah reached up and kissed him on the mouth.

'Like you said,' she whispered, 'I've been missing for six months. A little longer isn't going to make any difference to Gerard.' But already she was making plans to put an end to her supposed disappearance, to put an end to her sham of a marriage.

Gareth sighed. 'I guess you're right. A little longer won't make much difference now. It's just that—' He broke off and Leah glanced up again.

'Just what?'

'You do realise we haven't used protection tonight, Leah. I can assure you I haven't given you any dreadful disease, but have you given pregnancy a thought?'

'Yes. It did cross my mind. Briefly. But it's not very likely. My period only finished a couple of days ago.'

'You're not on the pill, then?'

'No. I used to take it, but I stopped when I left Gerard. He didn't want to have children yet, you see,' she said bitterly, thinking how he'd said he wanted her all to himself for a while. Wanted more time to brainwash her totally to his wants and needs, more like it!

'Well, I want children with you, Leah,' Gareth assured her. 'And as soon as possible.'

'You don't want to wait till we can be married?'

'No,' he said abruptly.

'A baby,' she mused, a warm, squishy feeling in her stomach. She would so love having Gareth's baby. 'But it's highly unlikely a baby will come from tonight. In a few days, maybe?' she said, looking up at him with love and hope in her face.

He stroked a possessive hand down her throat and over her still erect nipples. 'Then in a few days we'll make love all night every night,' he promised thickly. 'But for now, just kiss me again, Leah. Kiss me everywhere. Take me away to that perfect place where nothing exists in this world but you and me, together.'

She did kiss him everywhere. With relish and at length, till he was groaning again.

'God, but I adore you doing that,' he rasped, his hand shaky in her hair. 'I can't tell you how it makes me feel. You do love me, don't you? Oh God... Don't stop... Don't ever stop...'

She did. Eventually. But only to take him inside herself, to take them both to that perfect world where nothing existed in the world but the two of them, together.

And it *was* perfect. Exquisitely so.

Leah remembered what Alan had said about knowing by morning which man she preferred, both in bed and out. There was no longer any doubt in her mind. It was Gareth she loved. *He* was the reality, her feelings for Gerard the illusion. That had just been an infatuation, a naive young girl falling victim to a dominating and wickedly attractive man.

But he would not have the power over her now he'd once had. She was sure of it. Now she was truly in love, with Gareth, who had all of Gerard's physical attractions and none of his flaws.

She stared down at him as she rode him, enthralled by the glazed passion in his face, enthralled by her own passion. She felt the pleasure concentrate within her once more, felt it gather, rise, twist, then shatter into a million pieces, her climax even more intense than any she'd experienced before.

'Oh. Gareth,' she cried, their bodies spasming as one. 'My love...'

He gathered her down to him, holding her close while his seed pumped deep into her empty womb.

She thought about how, in a few days' times, that womb would not be so empty. Hopefully, a tiny egg would be waiting for him, waiting to burst into a new life.

Such thinking reinforced her resolve to have done with Gerard by then, to have severed that tie once and for all. She wanted to conceive Gareth's child with nothing hanging over her head, or his, wanted him to be as sure of her love as she was of his.

'I love you,' she murmured, and embraced him back. 'Love you,' she repeated endlessly, till she fell asleep in his arms.

CHAPTER TWELVE

'SUCCESSFUL night last night, I presume?' Alan said when he picked her up the following afternoon for work. He'd been discretion itself when he'd arrived at the boat that morning and ferried them both to shore. None of that 'wink-wink, nudge-nudge, say no more' stuff which Leah had been dreading.

'Pretty good,' Leah understated.

Alan chuckled. 'You're a cool one, Leah, I'll give you that. But, looking at that poor wrecked man this morning, I'd say it was more than "pretty good". Are you seeing him again tonight?'

'Yes.'

'Well, I hope you gave him the opportunity to catch up on some shut-eye today. We chaps do have a limit, you know, especially once we're over thirty. Not like these randy young bucks who can oblige every ten minutes.'

'Alan!' she protested, trying to look shocked through laughing eyes. Little did he know it, but Gareth would have given any young buck a run for his money last night. But he *had* looked a little weary by the dawn, and after dropping her home had gone back to his apartment for a long sleep. She'd tried to do the same, but had woken after only a couple of hours, her mind already racing with her plans for the following day.

'I hope you're being careful,' Alan said suddenly, and Leah's heart leapt.

'Careful? What do you mean?'

'Well, you don't really know this Gareth guy, do you? I mean…you only know what he's told you about himself. That's the way when you meet someone on holiday. Believe me when I tell you I've met some seemingly nice ladies in my day who spin you the most incredible yarns just because they're away from home.'

'Gareth would never lie to me,' she said firmly.

'What makes you so sure of that?'

'I just know it.'

Alan shrugged. 'Don't say I didn't warn you.'

'I won't have to.'

'Some women never learn,' he muttered under his breath.

'That's not fair. Gareth is nothing like Gerard. You yourself said I would learn a lot from spending the night with him. And I did. I know now what love is. I know what I want in life, and in men. I've been running away from both and it's got to stop. Which leads me to ask a favour of you, Alan.'

'Oh? What kind of favour?' he asked warily.

'I'm going to tell Gareth that you've got a day cruise booked for tomorrow and you'll be picking me up for work at nine-thirty.'

'Why? Where will you really be?'

'In Brisbane, asking Gerard for a divorce.'

'Without telling his brother?'

'Yes.'

Alan shook his head. 'Nothing good comes of lies, Leah.'

'It's not a bad lie.'

'There's no such thing.'

Her face hardened. Alan just didn't understand. 'Will you do it for me, or won't you?'

'What exactly do I have to do? I don't quite understand my part. After all, you can tell Gareth whatever you like. We're not likely to run into each other.'

'You might.'

'So you want me to make myself scarce for the day, is that it?'

'Yes. And could you possibly drive me to the airport?' The plane fares and a night in a Brisbane motel would take every cent she had in her bank account.

'At nine-thirty?'

'Yes.'

'Okay.'

'Oh, Alan, you're a doll!'

'More like an idiot. When will you be back?'

'In time for the cruise the following night.'

'You'd better be.'

'I will. I promise.'

Guilt consumed Leah the moment the lie was out of her mouth. She was in bed with Gareth at his apartment, her body still humming from his impassioned lovemaking when she braved the issue of where she would be the following day.

'You'll be gone *all* day?' Gareth said, disappointment in his voice.

'I'm afraid so.'

'What about tomorrow night? Will you be free for dinner?'

'I'm not sure. We don't have a sunset cruise on *The Zephyr* on Mondays, so day cruises on Mondays sometimes linger on into the evening. I…I'd better not promise anything. Look, I'll ring you when we get back, okay?' She was planning on ringing him anyway, from Brisbane, *after* she'd seen Gerard. She would have to if he wasn't going to worry, since she wouldn't be back in Broome till Tuesday.

'I guess that'll have to do,' he said disgruntledly.

Leah's guilt increased. It was awful deceiving the person you loved, but she was determined. It would be all for the best in the long run.

'Why don't you book one of the day tours around Broome?' she suggested. 'They're very good. If you ring down to Reception they'll book it for you. Oh, maybe not. It's a bit late.'

The wall clock said nine-thirty. Gareth had brought her back here to his place supposedly to cook her dinner—a thought which had intrigued her—but they'd ended up in bed before a single bite had passed their lips.

'I wouldn't want to do that, anyway,' he said. 'Group tours are not really my thing. I'll just potter around by myself, look at the scenery, check out the dinosaur prints.'

'Oh, those! Well, I think I should warn you that the ones you can see are not real ones, you know. They're duplicates. The real ones are out under the water line. I think you can occasionally glimpse them at low tide.'

'No matter. I just want to see how big they are. Fancy something to eat yet?'

'You can really cook?'

He grinned. 'Do you doubt it?'

Her own smile was sheepish. 'Er...I haven't had much experience of men cooking.'

'You mean Gerard, I suppose,' he said drily.

'Not just him. My brothers didn't cook, either.'

'I'm no great shakes, but I can grill a steak and throw a salad together.'

The telephone ringing out in the living room brought a scowl to Gareth's face and a frown to Leah's.

'Who could be ringing you?' she asked.

'Lord only knows.'

'Do you want me to answer it?' she offered. 'I have to go to the bathroom anyway.'

'No, no, I'll do it.' He threw back the sheet and jumped out of bed, striding over to yank open the double sliding doors which separated the bedroom from the living area.

Leah frowned as she watched his irritated body language. He wasn't quite as laid-back a person as she'd first thought, though not nearly as short-tempered as Gerard. Still, she supposed his passion had to come from somewhere.

He swept up the receiver, his back to her, his shoulders a little tense. 'Yes?' he snapped, then just listened for a while.

'Yes, it's very nice up here,' he went on briskly at last. 'No... No, I won't be back for a while... Look,

I'll call you next week and give you a definite date…
Yes, yes I do know that… Goodbye.'

He put the phone down slowly, thoughtfully.

'Who was that?'

'What?'

'I said, who was that?'

'My secretary. She wanted to know when I'd be
back in Brisbane. I'd rung her, you see, saying I might
be extending my stay.'

'Are you needed back at work?'

'They can cope without me. I have good staff.' He
walked back to the bed, sitting down on the edge and
resting a gentle hand against her cheek.

'Now that I've found the love of my life, I don't
want to risk it by rushing back to Brisbane. I want
you all to myself for a while.'

Leah found it ironic that he should say the identical
words she suddenly remembered Gerard had said to
her once, but with such a different intention.

'You just want to get me pregnant, don't you?' she
said, covering his hand with hers and smiling up at
him.

'Do you mind?'

'Heavens, no. It's what I've always wanted, to be
a mother. I'm no career girl, I'm afraid.'

'You'll make a wonderful mother.'

Her heart turned over at the love and admiration
which shone from his eyes. She drew his hand round
to her mouth and kissed it softly. 'And you, my dear-
est,' she murmured, 'will make a wonderful father.'

'I hope so,' he said. 'God, I sincerely hope so.'

Alan's warning about her not really knowing

Gareth slipped into her mind. 'There…there's no reason why you shouldn't be, is there, Gareth?' she asked
a little worriedly.

'Not really. No. Dad was a very good father, so I
have a good example to follow. I was more thinking
about our chances of conceiving a child together. Not
everyone has a baby just because they want one.'

'Yes, that's true. But we're both healthy. And I'm
young. They say girls are more fertile when they're
young.'

'Yes…yes, that's true.'

'And there's no real rush, is there? It won't matter
if we don't make a baby straight away. I mean…I do
love you, Gareth, don't get me wrong, but we *have*
only just met. I know it seems like we've known each
other for ever. At least, that's how I feel about you.
But the truth is we haven't. A few days ago I didn't
even know you existed. And vice versa.'

'No,' he denied, his eyes boring into hers. 'That's
not true. I *did* know you existed, Leah.'

The blood began draining from her face.
'What…what do you mean?'

For a moment, one terrible moment, she thought he
was going to say something which would spoil all
their happiness, their love for each other. She knew
she could not have borne that. Not after what Gerard
had done to her.

'Nothing bad,' he insisted, his eyes pained as he
took both her hands in his, his fingers caressing upon
her. 'I just meant I always knew a girl like you existed
for me somewhere. That's why I waited, why I never
wanted anyone else as my wife, or as the mother of

my children. I was waiting for you, Leah. Always you.'

'Oh, how sweet!' she cried, tears flooding her eyes as relief flooded her heart.

'No, it's you who are sweet, my darling,' he murmured, cupping her face and kissing her mouth. 'I love you so much. Always, remember that. Always always remember that.'

He kissed her again, and it was the sweetest, most loving kiss in the world. It soothed her soul while arousing her body. Suddenly she needed him as she had never needed him before, needed him to show her his love for her, to wipe any lingering doubts from her mind that he was the man she wanted to spend the rest of her life with.

They didn't get round to eating that steak and salad till much, much later.

Gareth dropped Leah home at eight-thirty the next morning, giving her enough time to be showered, changed and ready for Alan's pick-up at nine-thirty. He was dead on time and she was at the airport in minutes, with plenty of time to check in for her flight.

She managed to control her nerves pretty well till she had her boarding pass in her hands and the trip to Brisbane suddenly became a ghastly reality. A vicious attack of butterflies claimed Leah's stomach and she almost turned and ran. The thought of actually coming face to face with Gerard once more was both horrifying and undermining to her resolve. A steadying cup of coffee made no difference. She was petrified. Only by reminding herself over and over that this would never get any easier did she propel herself onto that plane.

When it landed in Darwin and her connecting flight to Brisbane was delayed for forty minutes, Leah almost backed out again. It would be late afternoon by the time she reached Eagle Farm airport. Five at least by the time a taxi deposited her at Sunshine Enterprises.

Not that Gerard would have left the office by then. He wasn't a nine-to-five person at the best of time. He'd never arrived home on a Monday till eight at least. Monday was his day for getting on top of things in the office. His letter, fax and phone day—catching up on everyone after the weekend and putting into motion things discussed with his sales and marketing team on the Friday.

Leah used to feel sorry for Enid on a Monday. She'd had to stay back even after Gerard left to finish what he'd dictated.

Workaholic slave-driver, she thought as she sat there in the terminal, waiting impatiently for the announcement to board.

As she waited, her eyes slid to the public phones dotted around and an awful thought intruded. What if for some reason Gerard *wasn't* in his office? What if his routine had changed during the last six months?

Suddenly Leah had to find out. Perhaps she was looking for an out, a reason not to go, an excuse not to face Gerard. No matter. She just had to know.

Jumping up from her seat, she hurried over to the nearest empty phone cubicle. She only had three dollars forty in change and hoped that would be enough.

Luckily, Enid answered her phone fairly quickly.

'Enid, this is Leah,' she said swiftly, her heart hammering away like a jackhammer. 'I can't talk for long. I don't have much money. Just tell me if Gerard will be in the office around five.'

'Yes. Yes, I see no reason why he shouldn't be. Why, Leah?'

'Because I'm going to be there around then. Maybe a little later. Only please don't tell him that. Promise!'

'I promise.'

'Thanks, Enid. I knew I could rely on you. Have to go. My money's running out.'

Leah hung up, her hands shaking.

She felt sick.

He was there.

She had no excuse not to go.

Oh, God...

CHAPTER THIRTEEN

LEAH'S nerves had reached unbearable proportions by the time the plane landed in Brisbane, her stomach revolving in eddies of nausea. As soon as she got off the plane she rushed to the ladies' room and into one of the cubicles, gagging as she leant over the toilet bowel.

Nothing came except a small amount of bile. Understandable, considering she hadn't eaten a thing all day.

Five minutes later she emerged from the cubicle, pale and shaky. She looped her overnight bag over her shoulder and struggled over to the washbasins, where a few splashes of cool water over her face and mouth made her feel marginally better. The large mirror wall above still showed dark-ringed eyes within her pasty complexion. Smothering a groan, she leant against the basin in front of her, her head drooping.

'You all right, dear?'

Leah's head jerked up and round to find an elderly lady looking at her with real concern in her kind eyes.

'Yes,' she croaked. 'Yes, I'm fine.'

'You don't *look* very well.'

'I'll be all right in a minute. Just a touch of motion sickness.'

'Well, look after yourself, dear. You're not getting straight back on a plane today, are you?'

'No. Not till tomorrow.'

'Then I'd take a tablet before you do, if I were you.'

'Yes, yes, I will,' she said, thinking to herself that there wasn't a tablet to cure what ailed her. She was on her way to see Gerard, her husband, the man she'd once loved to distraction and whom she'd thought she was over, had thought she could face without any danger of breaking down, or worse…of feeling anything in any way for him at all.

Now she wasn't so sure. Her head was whirling with so many ghastly possibilities. What if she took one look at him and felt what she used to feel? What if, with one fell swoop, her love for Gareth was smashed to pieces, if *he* proved to be the illusion, not Gerard?

Common sense told her that couldn't be. She loved Gareth. She knew she did. He had the sort of qualities she respected and admired. He was a warm, caring human being, whereas his brother evoked nothing but contempt for his cold-blooded ways.

Stop acting like a little ninny, she lectured her reflection in the mirror. Pull yourself together! Get a grip! Keep reminding yourself what he did to you. Any superficial physical attraction you might feel for him will be just that. Superficial. Think of him as nothing more than a reflection in a mirror.

Gareth's reflection. He might look the same as Gareth, but he's nothing like him. *Gerard's* the illusion. Always remember that.

Leah straightened her spine, breathing slowly and deeply. Gradually her head cleared and her eyes focused on her appearance. Too young-looking, she decided.

Balancing her bag next to the basin, she rifled through to find her brush and make-up bag. A few minutes later her reflection got the nod of approval. Much better. Her hair up in a sophisticated knot. Her green eyes rimmed in black. Red lipstick on her mouth.

She looked five years older already.

Pity about her clothes. Blue jeans and a red T-shirt were hardly power-dressing, despite the colour. She could have done with the red linen Chanel suit hanging in her wardrobe back at Kangaroo Point. Now *that* would have been power-dressing at its best!

Power...

That was the word which worried Leah the most.

Not love. Power. She could reason it was Gareth she loved, and not Gerard. But what of the power Gerard had once had over her, the power of his personality, his sex appeal, his ruthlessness? The very things which her mind told her she now hated had once enslaved both her senses and her will. She had been putty in his hands. No doubt about that.

But that was then and this is now, she reaffirmed as she moved from the ladies' out to the taxi rank. You're a different person after six months fending for yourself all over the world. You're stronger, more independent, more assertive. You know what you want out of life and it *isn't* Gerard. He was a hopeless husband and he would have been an even more hopeless father, whereas Gareth will be perfect as both! Time to seize the day, darling. Time to finish with the past and forge your own future.

Leah's courage and resolve remained strong till she stepped out of the taxi and walked into the cavernous foyer of the glass skyscraper which housed Sunshine Enterprises on its breathtakingly imposing top floor. At that point both began to dissolve. She managed to hold onto a modicum of composure in the lift, which was just as well, for as the lift doors whooshed back on the top floor she was met by a potentially undermining situation.

Several of Sunshine Enterprises' employees—whom she knew by sight—were standing there, waiting to take the lift down. It was, after all, just after five, departure time for most of the general office staff, only the executives and their PAs regularly working overtime. They all gawked at Leah. She wished the floor would open and swallow her up.

Still, their gawking served to put some much needed gelatin in her knees, and steel in her spine. With a cool smile, she stepped out of the lift and strode off down the plushly carpeted corridor which led down to Gerard's suite of rooms.

The false show of confidence had a welcome effect on Leah. She actually began to *feel* more confident as she moved along with her head held high, firmness in her step. She wasn't just pretending. It was a wonderfully reassuring feeling, and it came at just the right time.

This building—with all its elegance and grandeur—had once had an overwhelming effect on her. She'd been *so* impressed by Gerard's lifestyle. Awed, even. Glancing around, she now saw the trappings of success for what they were. Traps.

Squaring her shoulders, Leah kept on walking till the deep blue carpet was finally blocked by grey double doors with a security intercom panel in the wall. Before five, these doors were always wide open and led into a huge reception area staffed by a cool blonde in her late thirties, whose job it was to keep impatient businessmen at ease while waiting for the chronically busy boss of Sunshine Enterprises to see them. Leah had always been jealous of Gloria, till she'd found out the glamorous receptionist was happily married with three sons.

Some butterflies returned as Leah pressed the intercom button, but she controlled them fairly well.

Enid's crisply efficient voice came through loud and clear. 'Is that you, Leah?'

'Yes.'

Leah heard the lock on the door click back.

'The door's open. Come on straight through.'

The spacious reception area was dimly lit, Gloria's wide semicircular desk starkly empty. The air-conditioning felt cold. Everything was quiet. So very, very quiet. Nerve-wrackingly so.

Gulping down the lump in her throat, Leah closed the door behind her and walked slowly towards the door which led into Enid's own spacious office. Those awful old fears crowded back during that relatively short walk, the same fears which had inspired Leah's flight in the first place.

Please, God, don't let me look at Gerard and feel

anything but contempt, she prayed. But more than anything, please, God, just let him let me go!

Worry that he wouldn't do any such thing halted her step in front of the door, her hand seemingly in slow motion as it moved towards the knob. Suddenly the door was wrenched open, Enid's normally composed face quite flushed. 'I was beginning to worry you might have run away again,' she said agitatedly.

Leah stiffened. 'I haven't come all this way, just to run away again,' she said with a large dollop of false bravado. 'Gerard still in his office?'

'Yes.'

'Oh.' No escape, then. She had to go in. 'Don't...don't leave, Enid,' she blurted out, all her bravado gone. 'Promise me. Stay right here so you can hear me if I call out to you.'

Enid's eyes widened. 'You're not frightened of Gerard, are you?'

'Don't you think I have reason to be? He's a ruthless man, Enid. You should appreciate that more than most. You've seen the way he operates. He's not a man to be crossed. Not a man who would forget or forgive lightly. I know that now more than ever,' she said bitterly, thinking of his relationship with his mother and brother, the way he had callously cut them both out of his life. 'He must be very angry with me. He probably hates me.'

Enid was frowning and shaking her head. 'Gerard does not hate you, Leah. He would never harm you in any way.'

'That's what I believed. Once. Just like I believed

he loved me. But I no longer take things at face value. I look beyond the façade these days.'

Enid sighed. 'I do hope so, my dear. I do hope so.'

Leah picked up the strange ambivalence in Enid's reply. 'I always thought you didn't like Gerard,' she said accusingly. 'That you believed I was a silly little fool for marrying him!'

'I have to admit I did.'

'Then don't start defending him now,' Leah said sharply. She was sick and tired of unlikely people defending Gerard. 'He's not expecting me, is he?'

'How could he be?'

'You might have warned him I was coming.'

'No. I didn't.'

'Good. Because I want the black-hearted devil to get a damned good shock when I walk in there. I don't want him having any time to get that devious mind of his working, thinking he can con me a second time.'

'I don't think for one minute he thinks that, Leah,' Enid said quite sadly.

Leah threw her an irritated look, whirled and stormed into Gerard's office before her temper cooled, along with her courage. All the wind was taken out of her sails, however, when Gerard glanced up idly from his desk at her dramatic entrance, his body language betraying nothing but the mildest of surprises. Not a trace of anger. Nothing but a wry acceptance of her sudden reappearance.

'Well, well,' he murmured, leaning back into his black leather chair and eyeing her slowly up and down. 'If it isn't Leah. My fugitive bride. To what do

I owe this change of heart? In your letter you informed me you never wanted to see me again.'

Leah swallowed, aware that her heart was racing in her chest. And no longer just from temper. Damn the man! Why could he make her feel like this?

One cool glance and she was trembling inside. It *had* to be old tapes, playing in her head, she reasoned desperately. She couldn't still be in love with him. Impossible!

But he *was* impressive, sitting there behind his long shiny black desk, looking breathtakingly handsome in a superb three-piece grey suit. His crisp white shirt highlighted his deeply tanned face, his wavy black hair slicked straight back with a little gel. He looked sleek and sophisticated and incredibly sexy. Leah despised the way her eyes automatically ate him up, the way her heart and stomach lurched at the sight of him.

'I haven't changed my mind about *you*,' she threw at him, self-disgust putting some added sting in her voice. 'I still think you're a cold-blooded bastard. But I've grown up since leaving you, Gerard. And grown-ups don't run away from life's problems. Which is what you are. A problem. Or should I say...my unfortunate marriage to you is the problem. I want a divorce. And I don't want any nonsense. I intend to get myself a decent lawyer, so if you're planning on making any trouble for me, then think again!'

'A divorce,' he repeated, arching his eyebrows before sliding forward on his chair, his eyes dropping to scan the papers on his desk. He began sorting through them, no longer looking at her. 'Very well, Leah,' he said offhandedly. 'A divorce you will have, then. And without any trouble. Is that all?' he asked, glancing up from under his dark brows, his blue eyes coldly expressionless. 'Or is there something else you want? Money, perhaps?'

'Not from you,' she snapped. But suddenly she did want to hurt him, as much as he had hurt her. My God, she would not be dismissed without giving him something to think about. Infuriated, she strode over to the front edge of the broad black desk and leant against it, leaning over so far that she was barely inches from his startled face.

'I've found a man who loves me. Who really, truly loves me. Who can give me all the things you could never give me, for all your damned money. He's just as good a lover as you are, Gerard. In fact, better, because when we make love it's a two-way thing, not master and slave, which was the only role you wanted me to play. Slave to your ego, your incredibly arrogant, insufferable ego. The man I'm with now is sweet and sensitive. A giver. A sharer. I love him so much I can hardly bear to be away from him for a minute. And the ironic thing is you know him, Gerard. Can you guess? Can you possibly guess? No? I'm not surprised. You really can't see beyond your classically sculptured nose, can you? Well, it's G—'

She broke off abruptly, her own nose finally registering the unmistakable scent which was coming from her husband's body. It wasn't sandalwood. It was...

'Pine,' she choked out, her eyes flaring as wide as her nostrils.

'What?'

'You smell of pine. Oh, my God... Oh, no...no...'

Leah staggered back from the desk, one hand on her throat as though to stop any nausea from rising past that point. Her devastation was cataclysmic. Total. It crashed through her like a great wave, washing away all her new hopes and dreams like so much flotsam.

For there was no such person as Gareth! She'd been right the first time. Gerard didn't have *any* brother, let alone a twin. The man who'd claimed he'd fallen in love with her at first sight, the man who'd convinced her he was everything his brother was not, the man who'd inspired her to such stunning intimacies was none other than her husband, Gerard.

The magnitude of his pretence was so great—the quality of acting so good—it was almost worthy of some admiration. But, dear heaven, the perfidy of it all.

'That bloody smell,' he muttered darkly, and lifted a pained face to her appalled one. 'Will you listen if I explain? Will you *try* to understand?'

Leah could not believe his blind stubbornness. His *stupidity*!

'*Listen?*' she managed in strangled tones, her face twisted into an anguished grimace. '*Understand? What kind of monster are you? Do you have any idea what you've done? Are you so blind to the feelings of others that you honestly think you can still find some way out of this...this fiasco?'

He stood up and started walking around his desk towards her, his face determined. My God, she thought despairingly. He's not going to give up!

Panic-stricken, she retreated till the backs of her knees came up against one of the large leather chairs facing the desk. 'Stop!' she ordered him before he could close the distance between them. 'If you come any closer, I'll scream!'

He stopped, his eyes full of a very real desperation. 'You *must* let me explain, Leah.'

'I don't have to do any such thing! And I'm not going to. God, but I despise you, even more than I did before. Your arrogance takes my breath away. Your lack of sensitivity is beyond description! What you did was not only dishonest, it was cruel. You created an illusion and you made me believe in it, made me fall in love with it. But the last laugh is on you. Because Gareth finally cured me of you, Gerard. I no longer love *you*. It's Gareth who has my love, body and soul. Yet Gareth doesn't exist. He's a myth, a make-believe man. A…a joke!'

'No!' Gerard blazed. 'He's not! He *does* exist. He's *me*, my better half, the man I was before my father died, the man I might have been if I hadn't closed my mind to the concept of love. I banished it from my heart, exiled it from my soul because I'd seen what it had done to Dad, and I knew how much I was like him, in looks and sensitivity.

'Love seemed so uncontrollable, and I hated that. So I trained myself to remain emotionally distant from everyone, to make every decision with my head and not my heart. I drew up a mental blueprint for the sort of girl I wanted to marry and when I met you, you seemed to fit that blueprint perfectly.

'You think I fooled you, Leah, but it was myself I

fooled. For I did love you…from the very first moment I walked down that pier and set eyes on your
sweet self. I just didn't realise it till you left me. My
God, I almost went insane from missing you. And
from remorse. You have to believe me, Leah. I *do*
love you!'

Oh, he was good, she thought bitterly. So incredibly
good. A conman extraordinaire. But not good enough!
If he'd loved her, he would have come cap in hand
and his heart on his sleeve with honest apologies and
a million means of retribution. But, no, he'd come
with even more deception, more lies, more manipu-
lations.

All Gerard believed in was having his own way.
She'd always known down deep that he would not let
her go easily, that he would move heaven and earth
to get her back. She'd fitted his bloody blueprint perfectly and he wasn't about to let such a prize get
away, not when she was so malleable, so damned gullible!

But even she would not have guessed he would go
to such ridiculous lengths. One reason she'd believed
in Gareth's existence was that she could not find a
logical reason why Gerard would do such a thing.

She stared at him now and wondered what he had
possibly hoped to achieve, both in Broome and here
today. It seemed that his act here in this office—before she'd realised who he was—had been designed
to send her back to Broome as quickly as possible,
back into the arms of his alter ego. But for what purpose? How long did he think he'd have been able to

sustain the act? Surely he would have had to confess in the end.

'Why?' she groaned, clutching onto her sanity by a thread. 'Why did you do it?'

'Good Lord, Leah, isn't it obvious?'

'No. No, it isn't obvious. I can't imagine what you thought could be gained by such trickery. When were you going to tell me the truth? Surely you didn't think you could get away with pretending you were Gareth for ever!'

'I did try to tell you. That night on the boat. But then you…oh, hell…' He raked his hair back from his face with frustrated hands, spinning away from her to pace angrily across the room then back again. 'I'd just dig my own grave further if I told you why I changed my mind at that point in time.'

Leah flushed at the memory of the intimacies she'd engaged in with him that evening. All in the name of love. All without protection.

'Oh, my God!' she gasped, an awful penny dropping. '*That's* what your plan was! To get me pregnant. That's what *this* was all about here, earlier on. You wanted me to go back. To Gareth. You wanted me to keep sleeping with him till I conceived. And then you would have had an extra lever, because you thought I'd come back to you if I had our child growing in my womb.'

'That wasn't my original plan,' he growled. 'It just happened that way. For pity's sake, Leah, try to look at it from my angle. You would never have listened to me if I'd come to you as myself. You would never have believed me if I said I loved you and needed you.'

She was shaking her head at him. 'Do you wonder why? Oh, God forgive you, Gerard. You're even more wicked than I thought. You'd do anything, *anything* to achieve your selfish ends, wouldn't you?'

Her distress reached overload and she burst into tears. When Gerard went to take her into his arms, she struck out at him violently, slapping him around his face, his shoulders, his chest, calling him all sorts of horrible names.

He just stood there taking it, not bothering to protect himself. Finally the horror of what she was doing sank in. She staggered back, eyes wide on the vicious red marks on his cheeks, the blood oozing from the corner of his mouth.

'Oh…' she groaned. And, whirling, she fled.

A startled Enid rose from her desk as Leah raced past. 'Leah, wait!' Enid called out.

'Let her go, Enid,' Gerard said in wearily defeated tones. 'It's hopeless.'

But Enid did not let her go. She hurried after her employer's distraught wife, joining her in a thankfully empty lift, pressing the 'close doors' button before Leah could protest.

'I don't want t-to t-talk to you,' Leah sobbed, tears streaming down her face. 'You lied to me when I rang you the other day. You said Gerard was in Brisbane and he wasn't. He was in Broome. And so was Nigel. That's how Gerard got back here so quickly. Because his jet was parked at Broome airport. You told Gerard I was coming today.'

'I did lie to you the other day, something which I found very difficult. But you took me by surprise and I really had no option. On top of that, at the time, I thought a little white lie was in your best interests. But I didn't lie to you today. I didn't tell Gerard you were coming. Only the Concorde could have got him from Broome to Brisbane quicker than you could jet down from Darwin. He flew out of Broome just after you.'

Shock had a way of focusing the attention, and drying tears. Leah sniffled and blinked, frowning her puzzlement. 'Then who told him?'

'Your boss did.'

'Alan? I don't believe you. My God, was he paying Alan to spy on me?'

'No, of course not,' Enid said, exasperation in her voice. 'You really do have an exaggerated opinion of Gerard's dark side. Believe me, I *do* understand that what he did looks bad. But once he thought of it, *nothing* could sway him. He's a man, you see. And men are given to action rather than words. He didn't seem to appreciate the pitfalls of such a pretence. He just saw a way of redeeming himself in your eyes and grabbed it with both hands.'

Leah's curiosity was beginning to override her devastation. 'How did he find out I was in Broome in the first place?'

'One of your brothers told him. Pete. He rang up one day out of the blue, said it was time you either got divorced or talked things through.'

Leah sighed. She'd never told her brothers the full story. She simply said the marriage hadn't worked out and she had to get away for a while. She'd made them promise not to tell anyone at all where she was while she was overseas and they'd agreed. They'd probably thought that promise no longer applied once she was back on Australian shores.

'Once Gerard knew where you were, he wanted to go straight to you, but he was worried sick over how you'd receive him. Then he came up with his famous twin plan. I warned him it wouldn't work but he just wouldn't listen.'

'He told *you* his plans?' Leah said with a mixture of surprise and suspicion. It came to her suddenly that Enid was looking a lot smarter these days, not the same dowdy middle-aged woman of six months before. She was dressing better and looking much younger.

'He did,' Enid admitted.

'Isn't that a little odd?' Leah said stiffly. Gerard had never been one to give confidences.

'There's no need to concern yourself about your husband and me, Leah. Gerard loves you and only you. But our relationship has changed somewhat since the accident, I have to admit. There again, *he's* changed. A lot.'

'I presume you're talking about the car accident with the truck?'

'Yes. It happened a week after you left, the day the private investigator reported he'd been unable to find any trace of you. Up till then, Gerard had been hard as nails, pretending to me that your leaving him was just a temporary hiccup in your marriage, putting round a silly story that you were unwell, cancelling social invitations on that pretext. But he seemed to suddenly see that you meant what you said, that you were never coming back to him. He broke down. It…it was quite terrible. You have no idea. I tried to stop him driving home that night. I asked him to come to my place. But he wouldn't. He said he had to be alone. To think. According to the accident report, witnesses said he ploughed straight into that truck. It wasn't the truck driver's fault.'

'Oh, no! You mean he…he…?'

'No, I don't think it was a suicide attempt. I think he was just…distressed and distracted. Nevertheless, he nearly died from a ruptured spleen.'

'Nearly *died*!' The words took a few seconds to sink in, but when they did, Leah went white. The thought of Gerard dead was horrendous…as was the reason behind her horror.

'You still love him, don't you?' Enid said.

Everything inside Leah welled up to deny it. But in the end she could not. For Gerard *was* Gareth, and Gareth she *did* love. Impossible to love one side of a person without loving the other.

'Yes,' she said resignedly. 'Yes, I guess I do.'

'Then go back and tell him so.'

'No!'

'Leah, don't cut off your nose to spite your face. Gerard has learned a lot from your leaving him. He's a changed man. He even contacted his mother. Er…do you know about her yet?' Enid asked hesitantly.

'Yes, Gareth tol—' Leah broke off, frowning as she recalled all Gerard had told her as Gareth. She remembered how he'd hoped she would be more understanding of his so-called brother's behaviour after she knew his background. But all she'd done was spout more hatred towards him.

Leah's heart turned over at the thought of her husband sitting there, listening to her vicious vow never to forgive him. It was no wonder he'd felt she would not listen to any explanations he had to offer as himself.

'Yes,' she admitted unhappily, 'I know about his mother.'

'That's good. Well, she flew over straight away with her husband and they had a lovely long stay together. She really opened his eyes, I think, to his many misconceptions about women and love. Whatever, I know for a fact that he's missed you terribly. And he *has* changed, Leah. Give him a chance to show you how much.'

Leah looked into Enid's honest face and began to appreciate what she was saying. The fact Gerard had gained his secretary's liking and respect was something. She'd seen the way Enid had once looked at him behind his back.

'Yes,' Enid said, nodding slowly. 'He's won me over. And he's wept on my shoulder. More than once.'

Leah's eyes rounded. Gerard...weeping? It was an unbelieveable concept.

'Not that he'd appreciate my telling you that. But a man who can weep for the woman he loves is a man worth going back to, I think. Not that you should make things too easy for him. You must never let men like Gerard take you for granted.'

Enid smiled encouragingly at Leah as she lifted her hand off the button which had been keeping the lift doors shut. They whooshed open, still at the top floor.

Leah hesitated.

'Go on,' Enid urged. 'Go to him.'

CHAPTER FOURTEEN

HE WASN'T in his office. He was in the adjoining sitting room, slumped in a corner of the chesterfield, a glass of whisky cradled in his hands.

'Gerard,' she said, from where she was hovering hesitantly in the open doorway.

He didn't look up, just swigged back half the amber-coloured liquid. 'Go away, Leah. I'll give you a divorce. And a generous settlement. But for now, just go away.'

'No. You wanted the chance to explain. You wanted me to try to understand. Well, here I am, and I'm prepared to listen this time. So damn you, Gerard Woodward, you're going to try to explain!'

His eyes jerked up to stare at her, his wretched face holding a touching mixture of surprise and hope. 'You really mean that?'

Straightening her spine, she strode into the plushly furnished room, crossing the deep-pile carpet to the granite-topped bar in the corner where she poured herself an even bigger whisky than Gerard was downing. 'You'd better believe it,' she said.

He frowned when she lifted the glass to her lips. 'You don't like whisky.'

'How do you know? I've changed a lot in the last six months. I've been a lot of places. Done a lot of things. Tried a lot of things. I've moved on from just

Chardonnay these days.' To make a point, she took a deep swallow of the whisky, not flinching when it burnt a fiery path down her throat.

In truth, she had never drunk whisky before, but Leah agreed with Enid on one score. If she and Gerard had a future together she had to take a firm stand and make him see she wasn't prepared to go back to being the amenable little wife type. Or the silly romantic fool who'd been taken in by his super-sweet super-caring alter ego.

Maybe there was some of Gareth in the new person Enid claimed her boss to be, but there was still a lot of the old Gerard. A true Gareth-type person would never have perpetrated such a deception in the first place. That was a Gerard course of action.

'I'm waiting for you to begin your explanation,' Leah said as she prowled around the room, sipping her drink.

'Then for Pete's sake sit down,' he ordered.

'No,' came her cool refusal, though she compromised by standing still next to the window.

'I don't know where to start,' he muttered.

'Anywhere will do.'

'You're not making this easy for me.'

'Why should I?'

'Don't try to be tough, Leah. That's not you.'

She stared at him across the room with glacial green eyes. 'If this is going to be your attitude, Gerard, then I'm leaving again.'

When he said nothing, she placed her glass down on the windowsill and headed for the doorway. He was up and blocking her exit in a flash, his face apologetic, his eyes pleading.

'Don't go, Leah. If you leave me again, I think I'll go mad.'

'No more mad than I did when I heard you say those terrible things six months ago! How do you think I felt then, Gerard? I was shattered. And then afterwards…when you came upstairs and I couldn't stop you making love to me…I…I…'

Leah could feel the tears pricking at her eyes, feel the hurt returning. 'I won't ever be like that again, Gerard,' she stated more firmly. 'If you truly love me, you're going to have to earn my love, not to mention my respect. It won't be given mindlessly ever again.'

He was looking at her with such feeling, and such remorse that Leah almost weakened. Oh, how she ached to throw her arms around him and rest in the warm haven of his strong male body.

But she didn't.

And she was glad she didn't.

'This isn't going to work,' she went on staunchly. 'It's too soon for me to listen to you with an open heart and mind. So I'm going back to Broome, and if you really want me you're going to have to come after me, but as yourself next time. And you're going to have to woo me and win me all over again. You're going to have to prove to me that you've changed, that you want a partner, not a puppet, that being a husband and father is more important to you than making money.'

'But it *is*!' he insisted fiercely, and was on his feet, blue eyes ablaze. 'I've hardly spent any time at work since you left me. Most of the time I was recuperating at home, thinking about you and me, about where I went wrong, about what I was going to do if I was ever lucky enough to find you and get you back. You and your love are worth more to me than all the success in the world.'

'I find that hard to believe, Gerard. You thrive on your work. You live and breathe being an entrepreneur.'

'Not so much any more. Ask Enid. She and Steve have practically been running Sunshine Enterprises by themselves this last six months. And very adequately too. I won't promise to give up the business entirely. Or go back to architecture. Oh, yes, that was true. I did train as an architect. But I never did like it much. I only went into it because Dad wanted me to. He had some crazy idea about my designing houses and his building them. We were supposed to become millionaires together...'

His voice trailed off and Leah's heart squeezed tight with sympathy for his suddenly sad eyes. He really had loved his dad.

'Anyway, being an architect is not for me nowadays,' he went on brusquely. 'But I *can* promise you I have my priorities firmly in order. Work will never be first with me in future. That place goes to you, and our children.'

'That's good, Gerard. But they're still just words at the moment. I'm sorry, but words won't do any more. I need proof. So I'm going now. And I don't want you to try to stop me.'

His eyes narrowed. They were very Gerard-like eyes. 'No kiss goodbye?'

'Definitely no kiss goodbye.'

'When's the earliest I'll be welcome in Broome?'

'I would leave it a while, if I were you.'

'How long's "a while"?'

She smiled a wry smile at him. 'Gerard. Just come when you think the time is right. And when you're prepared to bare your soul to me as well as your body. Okay?'

'All right.' And he smiled back.

It was the hardest thing she'd ever had to do, walking away from him. Even harder than leaving him the first time. But she did it. Leah felt proud of herself. She hoped Gerard felt proud of her too.

The night spent alone in a motel room not far from the airport gave her plenty of time to think. She couldn't go to sleep for starters, too many thoughts tumbling through her head.

As she lay there, looking back over the last few days, the whole thing seemed so incredible! Yet Gareth being Gerard explained so many of her instinctive reactions to him, not least her instant and intense desire. Her eyes and mind might have been fooled but not her body. It had known its mate instinctively. She'd never stood a chance of holding out on 'Gareth'.

And Gerard had known that. My God, she'd confessed her sexual vulnerability to him to his face, had told him everything! She'd virtually handed herself to him on a silver platter from that moment.

As for all those sneaky answers he'd given to her many questions…

He'd deviously played with words and the truth. Of course he hadn't had a wife hidden back in Brisbane. She'd been sitting right in front of him! And of course Gerard would never have dared ruin Gareth's business, when they were one and the same!

For a while Leah was stirred by feelings of anger and chagrin over being made a fool of, but gradually any feelings of distress over what Gerard had done gave way to a reluctant admiration. What boldness he had! What daring! What a man!

Perhaps he *had* changed, as Enid had said. Perhaps he *did* really love her. Love was blind, wasn't it?

For, let's face it, Leah reasoned. Perpetrating such a deception was an act of manic desperation. Anyone with a brain in their heads could see it had been heading for disaster from the word go. The old Gerard would have relied on his silver tongue to talk his way out of trouble, not plunged in with a mad plan to pretend to his wife to be his own twin brother!

Leah couldn't help it. She started to laugh.

By morning she almost went back to see Gerard, stopping herself just in time. Enid was right. Things came to men like Gerard too easily. If she gave in without making him fight for her, he might soon forget to value her love, might start taking her for granted again. That would never do, not after all she'd gone through.

Still, she had to literally force herself to catch the early-morning flight to Darwin, then the connecting flight to Broome, a slight depression descending by the time she arrived. Already she missed him.

Missed him?

Leah frowned as she walked from the small iron-roofed terminal. Which 'him' did she miss? Gerard? Or Gareth?

Both, she finally accepted. She loved them both.

She smiled a drily amused smile. Not too many women could say they'd had an affair with their own husband. Yet she had. And she'd enjoyed every exciting and highly erotic second! When Gerard succeeded in winning her back—and Leah didn't doubt he would—that was one aspect of her marriage which was going to be irrevocably changed. She had no intention of being Gerard's sex-toy wife ever again. They were going to be partners in every aspect of their life, the bedroom included.

'You're looking pretty satisfied with yourself,' was the first thing Alan said when he picked her up at three-thirty. 'I presume things went well in Brisbane?'

'Much better than I thought, actually.'

'You mean the nasty old ex agreed to a divorce without kicking up a fuss?'

'Well, yes, he did, actually, but…er…um…'

'Look, there's something I have to tell you before you find out.' Alan interrupted her dithering before she could think of a way to explain the impossible situation. 'I had to tell Gareth where you'd gone. He was out on the point looking for those stupid dinosaur prints when I drove back from the airport. When he saw you weren't with me, he was like a dog with a bone till he got the truth out of me. Sorry.'

'It's all right, Alan. Gareth was bound to find out sooner or later, believe me.'

'Yeah, well, that's what I thought. You seeing him later tonight?'

Leah hesitated. Alan was going to think they were crazy if she told him the truth. Perhaps it would be better if Gareth just quietly disappeared from the scene, to be just as quietly replaced by Gerard when he showed up. 'Er...no, I'm not,' she said. 'Gareth's going back to Brisbane, Alan. It...um...didn't work out between us.'

'Oh, blow it! I thought you and he looked real good together. But I did warn you, Leah. You should have told him the truth. You know what they say... ''Oh what a tangled web we weave, when first we practise to deceive!'''

Leah couldn't agree more, though this 'tangled web' was beginning to be a fraction funny. Yet revealing all at this point in time was beyond her. She just couldn't face any more drama today. It had been a long two days. 'Would you mind if we didn't talk about Gareth any more tonight, Alan?' she said wearily. 'I'm pretty tired.'

'It's just as well we only have the one chap for the cruise tonight, then. He booked a private party, just for himself. Some people have more money than sense, don't they?'

'Maybe he's a photographer,' Leah suggested. Photographing Cable Beach sunsets was big business. 'You know how they don't like to share any vantage point.'

'Yeah. I didn't think of that.'

Once on *The Zephyr*, Leah went through the motions of making snacks for one, yawning here and there. Last night's largely sleepless hours were catching up with her.

'Our man's arrived on the beach,' Alan called out, just as she was covering the one small serving plate with plastic wrap. 'I'm off to pick him up.'

Leah went out on deck a couple of minutes later, listlessly waiting for Alan to return. She closed her eyes and let the rocking of the water soothe her sudden exhaustion, not opening them till she heard the motor approaching.

The sight of Gerard sitting in the back of the boat stunned her at first. It certainly propelled her out of any lethargy. She stared at him and he stared right back, his blue eyes watchful on her shocked face.

Alan jumped onto the deck, rope in hand, smirking as he bent down and whispered in her ear. 'It seems dear old Gareth isn't going back to Brisbane just yet. Neither did *he* want to share.'

'That's not Gareth,' Leah informed him resignedly. 'That's my husband. Gerard.'

'What? Oh, Good God, I'm not going through that rubbish again. That…is…Gareth,' he said slowly, pointing to her husband and rolling his eyes at her as though she were a moron. 'For pity's sake, show her the scar again, man. Geez, Leah!'

Smiling ruefully, Gerard stood up and showed her the scar.

'See?' Alan scorned. 'It's Gareth, not your nasty old ex. Now, can we just get on with this cruise without any more melodrama? Lord, the girl is paranoid!'

Leah had to smile. It really was funny.

'Shall we tell him the truth?' Gerard whispered as he came aboard.

'I don't think so, do you?'

'No. Because if we did, he might wonder why your nasty old ex is kissing you, and why you're not scratching and spitting.'

Leah didn't have time to protest before his mouth covered hers. She didn't scratch or spit, but she did stiffen for a split second. But then she relaxed, and melted into the man she loved. It was what she wanted, after all.

'You didn't waste much time,' she murmured when he finally let her come up for air.

'"Time and tide waits for no man,"' he quoted. 'I love you, Leah. I wanted to start proving it as soon as possible.'

'And you think kissing is the best way?'

'It's a damned good start.'

He was right, she thought blissfully. It was.

So she kissed him back.

EPILOGUE

LEAH circled the large living room, carrying a tray full of *hors d'oeuvres*, smiling and chatting to her many guests. Over two hundred, they spilled out onto the terrace and around the pool. It seemed nearly everyone in Hidden Bay was there to celebrate their house-warming party, including Leah's brothers and their fiancées. Leah's marriage and baby had finally inspired those two seemingly confirmed bachelors to tie the knot.

The house had taken a year to build, but was worth it, Leah thought as she glanced around. Light and bright and breezy, with tiled floors and comfy cane furniture, it was the perfect getaway from their busy Brisbane lifestyle—a place where they could relax as a family, and with friends. They already planned to spend every second weekend there, not to mention Christmas, Easter and all school holidays.

Not that school holidays would come into their lives for a while. Lewis was only five months old as yet, and Leah's second pregnancy was merely a date ticked on the calendar.

But time flew when you were happy, Leah knew. It was nearly two years since Gerard had set to winning her back. Two wonderful but unbelievably quick years during which she and Gerard had cemented a relationship—and a trust—which Leah felt confident would last for ever. They were best friends as well as lovers. Not only was their flesh as one, but so were their minds and hearts.

A man's hands suddenly came to rest on her waist from behind, pulling her over into a corner. Leah didn't have to turn round to know who they belonged to. Aside from anything else, she instantly recognised that tangy pine smell which she'd come to love even more than the other one.

'You just *love* serving food, don't you?' Gerard whispered in her ear, and she laughed.

'Alan's arrived,' he added.

'Oh, how marvellous!' she exclaimed, whirling round. 'I was hoping he'd make it.'

The three of them had become firm friends during the six weeks Gerard had spent in Broome, winning and wooing Leah all over again. Alan had laughed himself silly when they'd eventually got round to telling him the truth about Gareth. He'd thought they were both mad! Which they were. About each other.

'Did he say he had any trouble sailing that old tub all the way here by himself?'

'Said it was a breeze. Apparently he dropped anchor earlier in the day, but took a bit of time cleaning himself up for our party. Said he didn't want to embarrass us by turning up half-naked and with a five-day growth on his chin. And guess what else?'

'What?'

'He took one look at Enid and made a bee-line straight for her.'

Shock flung Leah's eyes wide. 'No!'

'Oh, yes! See for yourself. Look out there on the terrace.'

Leah looked and Gerard was so right. A surprisingly overdressed Alan was chatting away earnestly with Enid and she was looking into his soulful brown eyes as though he was a visitation from heaven.

'I shouldn't be surprised, I suppose,' Leah said ruefully. 'Enid's looking darned good these days. She's lost so much weight and she looks great as a blonde. Much better than that mousy brown. But still, she *is* nearly fifty! And I don't think she's been with a man since she left her husband about fifteen years ago.'

'Then it's about time, don't you think?'

Leah thought about it. 'Yes. Yes, I do!'

'Then I suggest you put down that tray of food and we'll take them both some champagne.'

'Good idea.'

It took several hours and several glasses of champagne before a besotted and somewhat sozzled Enid let Alan sweep her out of the house and off to a night of decadence aboard *The Zephyr*. Leah watched her go with some trepidation but Gerard chuckled and told her not to be so silly.

'Are you absolutely sure we did the right thing?' Leah reiterated after the guests had left and the house was quiet. She'd checked on Lewis, who was blissfully sleeping. A big and contented baby, he'd been sleeping through the night for a few weeks. 'Alan's not into love, you know, just lovemaking.'

'A good dose of lovemaking is exactly what that lady needs,' Gerard pronounced firmly. 'And speaking of a good dose of lovemaking...'

His blue eyes narrowed and darkened as his fingers slipped the straps of her nightie from her shoulders. It pooled on the floor at her feet, leaving her naked and instantly breathless. Her heartbeat quickened when he trailed the backs of his fingers across her breasts, their darkened areolae and distended nipples extra sensitive since breastfeeding Lewis.

'Did I or did I not notice that today's date had a tick against it?' Gerard murmured, bending to take one of those nipples, and then the whole areola, into his mouth.

'Yes,' she croaked, cradling his head against her breast and urging him to suckle harder. The sensations were incredible. Erotic and primitive. She abandoned herself to them, and to him.

He straightened to cup her face and kiss her hungrily. 'Tell me you love me,' he insisted between frantic feverish kisses.

She told him, as she told him every time they made love these days. He seemed to need to hear her say the words almost as much as he needed her body's responses. And she gave him all he needed, as she always did, gave it with all her heart and soul. For she loved him with all her heart and soul. Always had, and always would.

Tropical cyclone Michelle gathered and raged off the coast that night, but it could not quite compare to the storm which raged in the master cabin on *The Zephyr*, or the tornado of passion whipped up in the master bedroom of the Woodwards' new weekender. A cyclone was, after all, a destructive force. Those other two storms were far more creative, leaving behind new life in one woman and new confidence in another.

Nine months later a daughter was born to Leah and Gerard. They called her Michelle and asked Enid and Steve to be her godparents.

The two new partners of Sunshine Enterprises were happy to oblige, stunning everyone at the christening by announcing their engagement. They were married six weeks later and, despite a ten-year age gap, remained madly in love and blissfully happy.

Have Your Say

You've just finished your book.
So what did you think?

We'd love to hear your thoughts on our 'Have your say' online panel
www.millsandboon.co.uk/haveyoursay

- 🌹 Easy to use
- 🌹 Short questionnaire
- 🌹 Chance to win Mills & Boon® goodies

Mills & Boon® Online

Discover more romance at
www.millsandboon.co.uk

- **FREE** online reads
- **Books** up to one month before shops
- **Browse our books** before you buy

...and much more!

For exclusive competitions and instant updates:

 Like us on **facebook.com/millsandboon**

 Follow us on **twitter.com/millsandboon**

 Join us on **community.millsandboon.co.uk**

Visit us Online   Sign up for our FREE eNewsletter at
www.millsandboon.co.uk